HOOP CITY

BALTIMORE

SAM MOUSSAVI

EPIC
Press

Baltimore
Hoop City: Book #6

Written by Sam Moussavi

Copyright © 2016 by Abdo Consulting Group, Inc.

Published by EPIC Press™
PO Box 398166
Minneapolis, MN 55439

Cover design by Nicole Ramsay
Images for cover art obtained from Shutterstock.com
Edited by Lisa Owens

LIBRARY OF CONGRESS CATALOGING-IN-PUBLICATION DATA

Moussavi, Sam.
Baltimore / Sam Moussavi.
p. cm. — (Hoop city)
Summary: Marcus is the latest football star at an athletically prestigious Baltimore
high school. But when he gets into a bad fight with a white player at a preseason
basketball tournament, racial tensions start to run high, will Marcus' anger ruin his
brightly lit future?
ISBN 978-1-68076-043-9 (hardcover)
1. Basketball—Fiction. 2. High schools—Fiction. 3. Inner cities—Fiction.
4. Teamwork—Fiction. 5. Young adult fiction. I. Title.
[Fic]—dc23
2015903972

To Marina, with a white butterfly fluttering just above her shoulder

ONE

"You don't ever want to be known as a snitch, hear?" Joe said. "Where we come from it's a death sentence."

"I know that," I said.

"You do?"

"Chris wasn't no snitch," I said.

Joe shook his head and wanted to say something, but he hesitated. He thought for a minute, blowing cold air out of his mouth.

"It don't matter if Chris was snitching or not, Marcus," he said.

He made a wide circle with his hand and waved it around to the blocks, corners, and row-houses along Fayette Street. The corners—Joe's corners—were dead at that time of the morning. But that would change once nine a.m. rolled around.

"What matters is that everyone around the way, everyone on them corners, they thought that he was snitching," he said.

"He wasn't no snitch," I repeated.

"How do you know?" he asked. "Yeah, you two used to be close, but that was back in the day. Can you be sure about it now? How you know that guy wasn't talking to the police?"

"Did you know?" I asked. "That's what I want to know."

I looked Joe right in his eyes. And he looked back into mine without speaking. There weren't too many other people in West Baltimore who could look Joe in the eyes and live to talk about it, but I was one of them.

"I gotta get to school," I said.

Joe looked down to his watch. "Yeah," he said. "You're gonna be late."

I rubbed my hands together to get them warm. It was no use. The chill in the air went through my sweater and jacket, straight down to my bones. I stood up off the stoop, cupped my hands around my mouth, and blew warm breath into them.

"You shouldn't ride with me," he said. "Especially now."

"I'm good."

"Call one of my people if you need a ride," he said.

He nodded back to his muscle standing right behind him—a tall, tough-looking guy with black eyes and big muscles underneath his black hoodie. Joe never left his house without muscle. It was too dangerous. There were too many eyes on him.

"I'll walk," I said. "It's only a few blocks."

"Lay back on all this crap with Chris, hear?" he said. "I'm lookin' into who got him. I don't need you and your temper startin' any crap, hear?"

"Aight."

"Got me?" he asked with strain in his voice.

"You got more important stuff to worry about. We all countin' on you."

"I got you," I said.

"Hurry up then, man," he said before walking away and getting into the back seat of a black Expedition that was idling at the end of the block. The truck had black rims and tinted windows. For as long I knew Joe, his favorite color was black. He liked black clothes, black guns, black cars, black women, black everything.

When the door closed, his driver pulled away from the curb and ripped down Fayette toward downtown and away from me.

I didn't want a ride to school even though it was freezing outside that morning. I walked through the corner at Mount and Fayette where Chris fell the night before. I looked down to see if any of his blood was still on the sidewalk, but the cops did a good job of cleaning it all up. There wouldn't be slinging on that corner for at least a week or two. It was too hot. The crews would have to change corners if they wanted to keep selling or they could just wholesale their G-packs for a while, at least until the heat from Chris's death cooled or until another guy fell on some other corner in West Baltimore, whichever came first.

Chris didn't have to go out the way he did though. I knew Chris. He was damn-near my brother when we were kids. For a while there, he and I were on the same path. We thought that sports were gonna take us both up out of the 'hood, but somewhere on that path we started splitting off.

———

I got to school right before the first warning bell rang. On the way to homeroom, my boy DeShawn from the football team nodded and stopped me in the hall.

"Yo," he said. "You hear what happened to Chris?"

His mouth stayed open in shock.

I nodded.

"I know you two used to be tight," he said. "How you doing with it?"

"It just happened, right?" I asked. "They found him last night outside the Cut-Rate on Mount and Fayette laid out on the sidewalk."

"When you hear about it?"

"Late last night. A couple hours after it happened."

"Who told you about it?" he asked.

"Joe."

DeShawn's eyes got big. The name "Joe" meant something where we came from.

"You don't think . . . " he said before cutting himself off.

"What?" I asked.

"You don't think Joe got Chris, do you?" he asked. "Chris been workin' Joe's corners for years and all of a sudden he gets shot up?"

I shook my head.

"Joe wouldn't." I said. "He knows Chris and me were close."

DeShawn thought for a second. "Yeah. You probably right. It makes you wonder though."

"I gotta get to class," I said as the homeroom bell rang. "I'll holla at you at practice."

The rest of the day was the same. People in the halls and in class asked me how I was doing with Chris's death. I didn't say much to anybody, but inside I was shocked that he was gone. I wanted to know who killed him and why. I couldn't wait until Joe found out who pulled the trigger.

I was born and raised in West Baltimore. The guys I knew at school pretty much grew up on the same streets I did. Where we came from, a male of my age did one of two things: play sports or stand out on the corner.

There wasn't a third option.

———

"Gather up!" Coach Watson said. "DeShawn! Tyrell! Hurry up so we can get out of this cold!"

The two of them hustled up and joined the circle, removing their helmets and getting down on one knee.

"That was a good, crisp, practice," Coach Watson said. "The game plan is set. All the work you guys have done since August—May if you account for passing camp and weightlifting—prepared you for this moment. It's all prepared you for Saturday night."

He paused for a second to look out at us.

"The Maryland state championship game," he said.

Everyone was quiet and looking up at him.

"Tomorrow is a half-day at school, so walk-through will be at twelve thirty. We'll have a team meal after that and then I'm gonna send you home early. I want you off your feet and in the house by nine, thinking about the game, about football, and the opportunity in front of you," he said. "No fooling around. Stay home and rest. And then Saturday, well, it's game day."

Coach Watson carried it straight with us. He *was* one of us. Born and raised in West Baltimore just like us. He didn't play politics or hold favorites and we liked that. It made us play harder for him. I know I did.

"Okay," he said. "Get home safe. I'll see you tomorrow after school."

The guys stood up and started leaving the field in small groups. A lot of them put their helmets back on because of the cold. There weren't any parents around for rides home. Coach set up two buses to take the guys home after practices and games. That was just another reason we liked Coach. He looked out for us.

As I walked off the field, someone tapped me on the shoulder.

"Marcus."

I turned around and saw Coach Watson.

"What's up, Coach?"

He put a hand on my shoulder.

"I didn't get a chance to talk to you today during school or out here before practice. How are you?"

I unstrapped my helmet and took it off.

"I'm aight," I said. "I guess."

"I know you two were close."

"We were . . . I mean, over the years. We didn't really hang out like we did when we was younger. He did what he did and I went my own direction. But whenever I saw him around the way, it was cool. It was always cool. I would never turn my back on him. You know what I mean, Coach?"

"I do."

We started to leave the field.

"It's still real fresh," he said.

"Yeah," I said. "I don't believe he's gone."

"If you need someone to talk to," he said, "I'm here. Come by the office tomorrow or call me anytime."

"Thanks Coach."

"I'm sure when it sets in, you'll start to feel the

anger bubbling up inside of you," he said. "But I don't want you going out there and trying to settle this. It's all a part of the game. All those boys out on the corners know there's a risk. Don't you be stupid."

I nodded, but I wasn't really hearing Coach. I didn't want another lecture about the corners like Joe's lecture that morning. I just kept my mouth shut and my thoughts to myself.

"You need a ride?" he asked.

"Yeah."

"Come on," he said. "Let's get out of this damn cold."

We jogged the rest of the way to his car and pulled out of the empty parking lot. We didn't talk much on the ride home. I didn't mind. I just wanted to think about Chris and where we lost touch.

TWO

"Mama!" I yelled after unlocking and opening the door to the apartment we shared.

My dad was up in Jessup serving a life sentence for murder. He worked with Joe when the two of them were coming up and Joe was on his way to being a player.

My mom didn't answer. She was out with her friends, as usual. I took a shower and went straight to the fridge to see if there was any food. As usual, there wasn't much, just pizza from the night before and the nasty-smelling Chinese carryout from two nights before. The pizza would have to do.

I sat down on the couch in the living room

and turned on our new flat-screen TV. My mom bought it the week before and I really didn't get a chance to use it because of being busy with football.

Three years before, when my dad went up to Jessup, Joe moved mom and me out of the projects in Winchester to Edmonson Village. He set us up with a brand new apartment and filled it with everything we needed. He also paid our rent and the note on my mom's new Lexus. On top of all that, at the end of every month Joe would hand me an envelope to give to my mom. That money would keep us going. Scratch that; it kept my mom's pockets full of cash.

I guessed that Joe felt like he owed that to my mom and me on account of all the stuff my dad did for him.

My dad being locked up didn't mean much to me. He never lived with us even when he was free. The only time I saw him over the years was when he came to one of my games or stopped by to drop a little cash on my mom.

Joe was more of a father to me than my real father ever was.

I heard my mom's high heels outside the front door and I heard her slip them off after she walked in.

"Ooh, them heels is killing my feet!" she said as she took off her coat and tossed it on the couch.

"Then why are you wearing them?" I asked.

"Because I look good in them," she said as she sat down next to me.

"Can you put some food in that fridge?" I asked. "I come home and want something to eat and all that's in there is damn day-old pizza and stank Chinese food."

"What's your problem?" she asked. "Oh, you hurt over Chris?"

"It's screwed up," I said.

"It is," she said. "But don't you go out there fightin' with them wild guys, tryin' to figure out who killed Chris. You got responsibilities, boy—to me and to Joe."

"To Joe?"

"Who you think paid for all this?" she asked with a wave of her hand.

"All this is because my father ain't no snitch," I said.

"You don't know nothin', boy," she said. "Joe cares about you. He sees the talent you have in sports and he doesn't want to see that go to waste."

I turned my attention back to the TV.

"Boy, listen to me!" she said as she grabbed the remote out of my hand and turned off the TV. "Promise me you ain't gonna go fight nobody over this thing with Chris."

"Everybody keeps telling me that I need to cool out over Chris getting killed—and I ain't even trippin'."

"Good," she said. "That boy was out there on them corners, and if he got dead, there's probably a good reason for it."

I didn't say anything.

"Part of the game," she said.

"You done?"

"Just promise me."

"I promise," I said. "Now give me the remote."

I tried to snatch it out of her hand but she pulled it away.

"Another thing," she said. "Next time you see Joe, tell him I need to holler."

"Why?"

"Because I want him to front a package."

"Not this again," I said.

In Baltimore, a "package" or "G-pack" was what we called a thousand dollars worth of dope or coke.

"Man," she said, "someone has to grind in this family."

"Joe pays for everything. You never even lift a finger," I said. "Hell, you've never worked a day in your life."

"It ain't enough," she said. "And until you make it to the NFL or NBA or whatever, and buy me a mansion, we need a little extra something. I mean, this is Baltimore. If you ain't grindin' on them corners, you ain't crap."

"I don't know when I'm gonna see him next," I said.

"When you *do* see him, just tell him I need to get up with him, hear?" she said before giving me a slap on the side of the head.

"Aight!" I said. "Get on my damn nerves."

She got up off the couch and stood over me. "You lucky you're good at sports. Cause if not, you'd be right out there on them corners just like your father. Just like Joe when he was starting out. Don't go thinking you're above anything just cause you can play a little ball."

I didn't respond. She left the living room, went into her room, and shut the door.

My mom talked a lot. I was used to it. Most of it didn't mean anything to me. She always tried to get me to talk Joe into fronting her a package. She always wanted more, but I never paid it any mind. We had enough money to live—more than enough. I was steering clear of that crap, and tried to steer her clear, too. I knew the game too well.

She was right about Chris though. He knew what he was getting himself into, being out on the corners. He knew the risks. If he got killed for snitching or for some other crap, that was a part of the game and I could live with it.

THREE

By the time I got to school the next day, Coach Jones—the varsity basketball coach—pulled me out of homeroom to talk.

"Hey Marcus," he said when I walked into his office. "Take a seat."

I sat down in a chair in front of his desk.

"Ready for tomorrow?" he asked.

"Yeah, Coach," I said. "It's been a long year and I'm ready to get that trophy."

"Great," he said. "I'll be there in the bleachers watching you."

I nodded.

"Praying you don't get hurt," he said.

"Nah, I'll be good," I said. "They can't hurt me."

"How much time do you think you need until you join the basketball team?"

I thought on it before giving my answer. My body was beat up from the football season and my mind wasn't ready for basketball yet.

"I haven't really thought about it, Coach," I said. "Last year we didn't even make it to the playoffs in football. This year . . . "

I shook my head.

I played varsity football and basketball the year before as a sophomore. Football was my first love; it was the first sport I ever learned how to play, and the football field was a place that I could take out my aggression and anger without getting into trouble. But basketball came easy to me and when Joe noticed that, he told my mom that I should play both. He told her that playing both sports would give me double the chance of making it to the pros and getting out of West Baltimore. From that point on, I played both.

"You tired?" he asked.

"Yeah," I said. "But I'm still gonna play basketball this season. Don't worry."

"Okay," he said.

I could see the relief on his face. I don't know why he was tripping. I never told anyone that I was even thinking of not playing basketball.

"Is that all?" I asked, standing up from the chair.

"We should decide when you'll join the team."

"I don't know," I said. "I could use a week off after the championship game on Saturday. You know, get my body right and clear my head."

"A week?" he asked. "I was thinking more like three days. You could take Sunday, Monday and Tuesday off and join us for practice after school on Wednesday."

"If you got it all figured out, then why'd you ask me what I thought?" I asked. "Just tell me when you want me to join the team and that's when it'll be."

"Okay, then Wednesday it is."

I nodded, slightly annoyed, and walked out of his office.

———

After walk through and the team meal, Coach Watson let us out at around five p.m. The weather was different than the day before. The sun was out and the cold air was gone. I decided to walk home instead of getting a ride. I wanted to walk through my old neighborhood and see if I ran into any old faces.

When I hit the corner of Mosher and Riggs, there were a bunch of familiar faces out there grinding. There was Little Rick, who was six-foot-three; there were Petey and Melvin—two guys that I grew up with and went to school with until they both dropped out; and finally, there was the crew chief, Byron. When I was younger, Byron, Chris, and me were a tight little crew. Whatever dirt we did, we did it together. And Joe would always be there in the background cleaning it up. Like with Chris, I lost touch with Byron as sports played a bigger role in my life.

I wanted to see if Byron and Chris were still tight though. I wanted to see how Byron was carrying Chris's death.

"Look at this Hollywood guy walkin' down this block!" Melvin yelled as I approached. "Shouldn't you be locked away until the big game tomorrow night?"

"What kind of off-brand, hill-top corner is this?" I asked with a smile. "The fiends can't even find y'all all the way down here." I pointed a thumb back in the direction from where I came from. "They done found their blast five, ten blocks that way."

Rick, Petey, and Melvin all laughed and then shook hands with me. Byron looked at me briefly, and then looked straight ahead.

"What up, Byron?" I said with a nod.

He nodded back to me and looked straight ahead again like I wasn't even there.

"You know, with all this stuff goin' down with Chris," Petey said, "we had to pack up shop and move all the way down here. Knockos out there bangin' us hard, whalin' on anyone who even standing out on a damn corner."

"Yeah, I saw that coming," I said.

"It's all good, though," Petey said. "Once this stuff cools down, we'll be back up on our regular spot."

I eyed Byron again and he was still looking straight ahead.

"But anyways, how you holdin' up?" Petey asked. "You got that championship game tomorrow night. I see you out there doin' your thing."

"I'm cool, man," I said. "You guys should come through to the game. I'll leave some tickets out at the gate."

"That's what's up," Melvin said.

"It's at the Ravens stadium, right?" Rick asked.

"Yeah," I said with a smile.

"We'll be there," Petey said.

"Y'all are talkin' too much," Byron finally said, *still* looking straight forward at something across the street. "Spread out. Knockos come down here and see this raggedy-ass crap, we'll all be in cuffs."

Rick, Petey, and Melvin got quiet. I could see how Byron carried his corner. I could see why Joe wanted him as crew chief. Byron was always tough. I remembered that about him. But the game had hardened him even more. There was no doubt about that.

"Yo, Byron?" I said. "Can I get up with you?"

He turned his head and looked at me with no emotion.

"Let's walk," he said with a tilt of his head.

I shook hands again with the other guys and they spread out. I walked over to Byron and we started down the block on Riggs.

"How you been?" I asked. "Been a long time."

"You know," he said. "It ain't no joke out here, but I'm gettin' by."

"Looks like Joe's treatin' you good. You're already in charge of your own crew."

He rolled his eyes at the mention of Joe's name.

"You are workin' for him, right?" I asked. "You are workin' his package?"

He nodded and fished for his pack of Newports in his jeans. He pulled one out and lit it, then blew some smoke up into the air. I could see something was on his mind—something weighing him down. I knew it had to do with Chris.

"How are you holding up with Chris's death?" I asked.

He smiled in my face and his eyes got real bitter. He took another puff of his cigarette and blew the smoke out quickly.

"How you think?"

"Have any idea who did it?"

"Yeah," he said. "I got an idea."

"Well, what's up?" I asked. "You gonna spit it out?"

He laughed and shook his head.

"I know we lost touch, B," I said. "Same thing happened with me and Chris. But you two were my boys. And this news with Chris . . . it was a shock. I mean, you always hear about some guy you knew at some point in your life getting killed out here. But this is different. The three of us go back a ways."

Byron just stared at me as he took another drag. He was looking past me just like when I walked up on his corner.

"If you know who did it, they need to get got," I said.

Byron threw his cigarette down on the sidewalk.

"Ask your man about it then," he said. "You don't need to go too far to get answers."

He started to walk away and I grabbed him by the shoulder and turned him around. "What the hell, man?" I asked. "What do you mean?"

He looked past me again. "Byron," I said, staring straight into his face until his eyes met mine. "What are you saying?"

"Joe," he said. "Joe killed Chris."

I shook my head and backed away. "He wouldn't . . . "

"No?" he asked. "You think that, right? But you don't believe it. It's just something you tell yourself to make it go down easy."

"It don't make sense," I said. "Chris worked for Joe. The only way Joe would do something like that is if Chris was snitching. And Chris wouldn't talk to the police."

"Don't tell me what I already know," he said. "Chris was like a brother. Closer to me than real brothers, even. He didn't deserve to go out like that."

"You guys were still close?" I asked.

He smiled bitterly. "We can't all play sports," he said. The smile went away. "We stayed tight. He had my back and I had his."

"Was he in your crew?"

"He was my number two."

"Where were you the night he got killed?" I asked. "If he had your back and you had his, I mean . . . "

"Chris ran the shop at night," he said, "for a few hours after the sun went down. And besides, nobody would screw with Chris. They'd know they'd have to answer to me."

"Nobody except Joe," I said.

He didn't say anything.

"I'm gonna ask Joe about it," I said.

"Stay outta this," he said. "I'll handle it. I'm just thinking on some things now."

"Let me find out for sure before you grab your whistle and start raising all kinds of hell out here," I said.

"Oh, I already got my whistle," he said as he raised his shirt to reveal his nine-millimeter. "Like I said, I'm just thinkin' on some things."

"You'll lose," I said. "You know you'll lose."

"Screw it, then," he said. "As long as I get Joe for doing Chris, it's worth it."

He started to walk away and I grabbed him by the shoulder again. I put a little extra force into it this time. He turned around, glared down at my hand, and then eyed me.

I let go of his shoulder.

"Just give me a couple days before you do anything," I said. "I'll talk to Joe—I won't tell him you and me spoke. How can I get in touch with you?"

"We don't use no phones," he said. "If you look hard enough, you'll find me." He started walking back down to his corner.

"Have fun at your game tomorrow night," he said without turning around.

FOUR

I woke up the next morning with a terrible taste in my mouth. After talking to Byron, I went out looking for Joe. I was one of the only people in the city of Baltimore who knew where to find him.

I checked all of his normal spots. His "office" on Pulaski, the back room of the barbershop on Edmonson and Brice, the main stash house on Poplar Grove and Terrace—a long shot—but nothing. He was nowhere to be found.

I left messages all around town for him to get up with me when he could. I called every number I could remember to get word to him. He never talked on the phone himself anymore, but hopefully he'd send word through one of his people.

I couldn't sleep at all that night. I needed rest for the big game, but my mind wouldn't ease up on me. I didn't want to believe that Joe killed Chris. He knew that the two of us went way back. He knew that would hurt me. I had to find out the truth.

Every time the phone rang at my house, I jumped on it. And every time it wasn't Joe, I hung up in frustration.

The game was at five o'clock. I asked my mom to drop me off at school around noon. We had to meet there as a team at one p.m. and then take the buses to the stadium. I would be early, but I had to get out of the house.

"Joe's gonna be at the game, right Mom?" I asked in the car.

"You know better than me," she said. "What'd he say the other day when you saw him?"

"He didn't bring up the game," I said.

We were silent as we drove down Fayette. The

weather was nice but the corners were still dead. Every other corner or so, I saw knockos wearing undercover clothes posted up in their unmarked cars. Either they didn't know or were too stupid to know that just a few streets over, deeper in the hood, the fiends were still copping dope and coke and the players were still making money hand over fist.

"He'll be there," my mom said as she stopped the car in front of school. "I'll see you after the game. Do your thing tonight. Love you, Baby."

She leaned over and kissed me on the cheek. I got out of the car and she drove away.

I walked around to the back of school where the buses were already waiting. The door to the locker room was open and I walked through it. Coach Watson and the assistant coaches were standing around talking. A few guys from the team were sitting in front of their lockers.

"Marcus!" Coach Watson said. "You're early. Everything good?"

"I couldn't wait anymore, Coach," I said. "I didn't know what else to do with myself."

He smiled. "It's not too much longer," he said. "Go take a seat. Relax."

A wave of tiredness hit me right then. It made sense with how little sleep I'd been getting.

"Actually, I'm gonna go take a little nap in the trainers' room," I said.

"Sure," he said. "I'll send somebody to come get you when we're ready to leave."

I lied down on one of the trainer's tables and closed my eyes. The biggest game of my life was hours away and my mind was somewhere else. I had to get my mind right and get focused. I hoped that all I needed was a few minutes of sleep.

———

It was a dream to play at the Ravens Stadium. That meant something big to a young male growing up and playing sports in West Baltimore. I had been there before to watch Ravens games—Joe took me plenty of times—but actually setting foot on the field would be a different experience.

When our buses pulled up to the stadium, I felt it for the first time. It finally sank in how far we had come. The rest of the guys were excited, too. Their eyes lit up even more when the bus stopped in front of the entrance to the Ravens locker room.

We got to change in the Ravens locker room because we were the home team for the championship game. The team we were playing was from Anne Arundel County, and just like us, they had only one loss during the regular season. They liked to run the ball and favored a physical style of play like we did. The main difference between our two teams was that they were mostly white. When I watched film on their defense during the week leading up to the championship game, I saw only three or four black players on the entire team, and only one of them got a lot of field time.

As soon we got into the locker room, I changed

into my football pants and cleats. I wanted to get out on the field and soak it in a little bit. The weather was still perfect. The sun was out and it was fifty-five degrees—way warmer than any other November I could remember. That suited me. I knew I was going to get the ball a lot during the game. Hopefully the warm weather, plus my punishing running style, would wear their defense down.

By the time players from both teams came onto to the field, I'd already broken a sweat. I was ready to go. I wrote "RIP Chris" on both of my cleats. I wanted to have a big game and get the win for him.

There was an hour to go before kickoff and the sun was just starting to set. The people running things switched on the stadium lights, and slowly the lights kicked into action. The lower bowl of the stadium was starting to fill out. They were expecting about twenty thousand people to show up for the game.

Coach Watson approached with a big smile on his face and his hand extended.

"What do you think?" he asked before shaking my hand and patting me on the back.

"It's a dream," I said.

"You'll get used to it," he said. "In a couple years, playing in front of twenty thousand isn't gonna mean much to you. You're gonna be playing in front of a hundred thousand on Saturdays in the fall."

"Thanks, Coach," I said. "Oh yeah. Can you tell someone to leave five or six tickets at the gate?"

"Old friends from around the way coming to check you out?" he asked.

"You know it," I said. "West Side, baby." I threw up the "dub" sign with my right hand.

"I'll have someone run up and leave the tickets," he said.

I nodded to the Mully Man blasting out of the stadium's speakers. I shook Coach's hand one last time before the game and went back to stretching.

"Do your thing today, Marcus," he said. "Today is your day."

"No doubt," I said.

FIVE

The lower bowl was packed right before the opening kickoff. There were some people in the upper deck too. And it was loud. I couldn't hear myself think. That was probably a good thing. I didn't want to be out on the field thinking too much. I just wanted to play fast and react.

I stood at our goal line waiting for the opening kickoff. I looked to each side of the field and saw two different cheering sections. Our side of the stadium was filled with all black faces; most were wearing hoodies and all were wearing jeans. Their side was pretty much all white, wearing sweaters with the collars of their shirts poking out from underneath.

The ball was kicked straight to me and I caught it at the ten. I made two tacklers miss and got the ball out to the thirty-yard line. The other team looked bigger in person than they did on film—a lot of big, strong white boys. I knew I had to break a lot of tackles or else we wouldn't have a chance.

On the first play of the game, we ran a toss sweep to the right. Their defensive line blew our offensive line off the ball and trapped me in the backfield. I fought off three tacklers just to get back to the line of scrimmage.

When we got back into the huddle, I stepped in front of our quarterback, Josh, and looked my offensive line in the eyes.

I ripped my mouthpiece out.

"Y'all need to step up!" I screamed, spit flying out of my facemask. "I know they're big! I don't care! Block them for one second and I'll do the rest! Just don't let them blow you off the ball, hear!"

I backed up and jammed my mouthpiece back between my lips. Josh stepped in and called the next play. It was a screen pass to the left. This was a bread and butter play for us all year.

Before the snap, my eyes scanned their entire defense. They were playing run all the way. Their defensive line waited for the snap of the ball in aggressive, track-runner stances. Their linebackers twitched with anticipation.

Josh called out the snap count and the center snapped the ball. The rush came quick. The D-line shot the gaps and the linebackers filled like hungry dogs. The play would be wide open if Josh could get the pass off. I put my head down and sprinted out into the left flat. Josh let the pass go just before one of the defensive linemen could bat it down. The ball hung in the air, and when it finally dropped into my hands, all I saw was green grass.

I took it straight down the left sideline, untouched all the way to the house.

Seventy yards.

Seven-nothing us, just like that.

Our sideline erupted with screams and then

dancing. The ladies shook their hips and butts, taunting the white girls on the other side with less meat on their bones. And the fellas threw up their "dubs" for West Baltimore.

When I got over to the sideline, I barked at our crowd to keep them hyped. The other side was quiet now. The preppies didn't have anything to say.

By the time we kicked the ball off to them, our crowd was still screaming and talking smack to the other side. When our defense ran out on the field, I found a spot next to Coach Watson.

He turned his head and gave me a sideways look. "You ain't playing defense today, Marcus," he said. "No way."

"But Coach," I said. "I'm good. My energy is up. I'm hyped. I can handle going both ways tonight."

"Nope," he said, turning his head back to the field. "Just offense tonight. We're gonna need you fresh. There won't be seventy-yard touchdowns on every drive."

Coach kept his eyes on the field as our defense

allowed a twenty-yard run on first down. He gritted his teeth and walked down the sideline as the refs moved the chains.

I followed him.

"At least let me get in there on passing downs, Coach," I begged. "I can rush the—"

"I said no!" he snapped and turned away.

I unbuckled my chinstrap angrily and put my hands on my waist. It pissed me off that Coach wouldn't let me go in on defense. I understood that he wanted to keep me fresh for offense, but this was the championship. We had to go all out if we wanted to get the win.

At the end of their first drive, the other team scored a touchdown on a ten-yard pass. They had used up the rest of the first quarter with their drive. The score was tied at seven when they kicked it back to us at the beginning of the second quarter.

Coach Watson grabbed me by the shoulder pads before the offense ran out on the field.

"We have to keep scoring, Marcus," he said. "I'm not sure our defense can hold them tonight."

"Maybe if you put me out on defense, we'll—"

He raised a hand to cut me off and I shut my mouth. The old me would have kept arguing with Coach until there was a blowup. The new me decided to take out my frustration on the other team.

"Keep the guys up in the huddle," he said with a smile and a pat on my helmet. "Especially the offensive lineman."

"Aight," I said before trotting out on the field.

After they scored to tie the game, our crowd was silent and theirs was up cheering. Before we snapped the ball on first down, I took my pre-snap read of the defense and realized that my seventy-yard touchdown from before was not going to stop them from being aggressive. Their linebackers were close to the line ready to stop the run, just like on our first possession.

I got stuffed for a gain of one on a run to the left.

After bringing me to the ground, their biggest linebacker stood over me. "I'm gonna be here all day," he said. "That touchdown was a fluke."

"I'm right here, baby," I said with a smile. "I'm right here."

I had a reputation for losing my cool and there were always at least one or two guys on the other team who tried to bait me. But I wasn't going to let it happen on that night. The game was too important. My team needed me.

On second down we tried another screen pass, this time to the right, but their defense was ready for it. On third and nine, we tried a toss sweep to the right, and I got five out of it. Coach decided to punt it on fourth down. They started their second drive at their own thirty-five-yard line.

I tapped Coach on the shoulder during the timeout after the punt.

"There's no room to run," I said.

"What do you think?" he asked. "Stick to the power game for another possession and see what happens?"

"I don't know. They're big up front. And strong."

Coach didn't say anything. He just stared out at the field.

"There's no time to waste, Coach. We can't be feeling things out. We gotta just go."

"So what do you think?" he repeated.

"Let's scrap our power runs," I said. "Put another receiver out there and let's spread 'em out."

"They won't respect our passing game," he said.

"I know," I said. "But if we spread the field, they at least have to space out a little. I just need some more room out there. It's clogged up right now."

The refs blew the whistle for the game to start up again.

On the first play, their QB faked a handoff to the right and threw a bomb down the middle of the field. Their receiver caught it in stride and they took the lead, fourteen to seven.

Coach looked at me after the play. "Okay," he said. "We'll put the extra receiver out there. Get you a little more room to run."

"All I need is a little daylight," I said. Their crowd was now as hyped as ours was after my first score. I looked over to our side as I waited at the goal line for the kickoff. Our fans were pouting now, looking scared and defeated.

I ran up to take the kickoff at our ten-yard line. I broke a tackle at the twenty and then cut back to the right. There was a small crease there and I hit it hard. I got to the sideline, almost at full speed, and would've taken it to the house if not for one of their guys barely pushing me out of bounds. We had it, first and ten, at their thirty-yard line. I looked over to my teammates on our sideline and pumped my fists and bobbed my head. Our crowd got loud again.

Coach Watson sent the extra receiver in and we now had a formation of three receivers, one tight end, and me in as running back. We had a lot of success that year with the power running game—pulling guards and all that old school Vince Lombardi crap—but this team was the best we'd faced, especially up front. We had to do something different or else we'd get blown out.

On first down, we tried a delayed draw to the left. There was a hole and I hit it for a gain of twelve. I took a pre-snap read before the next play. Our new formation put them on their heels. Even though we weren't known as a passing team, they had to at least move a guy out to our extra receiver. That created the little extra space I was looking for.

We snapped the ball and Josh handed it to me on a quick trap play to the right. I broke an arm tackle two yards past the line of scrimmage and carried the ball down to their five-yard line. Our sideline cheered and got rowdy again. Coach Watson turned around to quiet them down.

On first and goal from the five, Josh faked a handoff to me going right and their whole defense followed me. By the time they realized that I didn't have the ball, Josh was running around the left side and ran untouched into the end zone. He spiked the ball into the air before the offensive linemen mobbed him.

The score was tied at fourteen with two minutes to go in the first half. Our sideline was free to cheer now and Coach Watson was leading the charge.

When I ran over there, he grabbed me with both hands by the helmet. "That's big!" he yelled over our sideline's cheers and taunts. "You just changed the whole damn game! That's big, Boy!"

Josh ran over to me and we both jumped at the same time for a chest bump. "Them white boys didn't even know I had the ball," he said.

"We do this together," I said. "Let's keep it rolling."

I ran over to the barrier between the field and the stands, and pumped our crowd up some more. I turned to look around the whole stadium and realized the entire lower bowl was packed. You couldn't see one empty seat. There were even patches in the upper level that were filled.

I had a quick thought about Chris and it almost made me shed a tear. He would have loved to see me make it. But I quickly put the thought out of my head. There was still more work to do on the field. There would be a lot more time after the game to think on my friendship with Chris.

We stopped them from scoring on the last drive of the first half. The score was still tied at fourteen when both teams ran back into the locker rooms under a wall of sound from the competing crowds.

I did some stretching in the locker room to keep loose. I tried again to get Coach to throw me in on defense, but he refused. He talked to the team briefly before splitting us up into our offensive and defensive groups. We planned to keep them off balance with the three-receiver formation and our power formation. On defense, we were going to blitz more often to rattle their passing game. Blitzing more would be a gamble. Our pressure would have to get there or else it'd mean one-on-ones with their receivers against our corners. I didn't like those odds.

It was their ball to start the half. We blitzed on the first three plays of the drive. And just like I thought, the results were high risk, high reward. On the first play, we sacked their QB for a loss of ten. But on the next two plays, they picked up our blitzes and gained fifty yards on two passes. They had first and ten on our thirty-five-yard line. They were in a power run formation now. We showed another blitz without disguising it. Their QB changed the play at the line with a hand gesture, and instead of a run, he faked the handoff and found one of his receivers down the left side for a touchdown. Their receiver had our cornerback beat by ten yards. It wasn't his fault, though. Our strategy was all screwed up.

I slammed my helmet in frustration. A few of the guys and an assistant coach tried to calm me, but I shrugged them off and paced down the sideline away from the team. I closed my eyes and took five deep breaths. During sophomore year, I had a blowup during a basketball game, and after, Joe told me to take five deep breaths the next time I felt the anger coming on. The next time I got angry during a game, I tried it and the five deep breaths calmed me down. I've used it ever since. It worked that night too.

We trailed twenty-one to fourteen after the extra point. I grabbed my helmet off the turf and put the missing parts back into their places. I walked over to Josh and gave him a fist bump.

"We gotta do this ourselves," I said.

"We got this," he said. "Those preppies across the field ain't never dealt with nothin' real. This'll be cake for us."

I nodded and ran out onto the field. I waited for the kickoff at my goal line, and because I hurt them badly on the previous one, their kicker sent a squib kick down the middle of the field. One of our guys up front fell on the ball as soon as it came his way. We took the ball at our forty-yard line.

As the rest of the offense jogged onto the field, I called out to their linebacker, the one that was talking smack to me in the first half.

"Y'all scared!" I said. "Why don't you tell your coach to stop being a sissy and kick the ball to me?"

"You ain't nothin'!" he said. And he repeated it a few times.

We stayed with the spread formation and I gained forty yards on five carries during the drive. The clock was already at one minute left in the third quarter. We had to score a touchdown here.

On first down from their twenty-yard line, they stuffed me for a loss of two. Their talkative linebacker was there again. I went to a knee as I got myself up off the ground. I needed a couple of seconds to catch my breath. The linebacker looked down at me with his hands on his waist.

"You tired?" he asked. "I told you earlier, you ain't nothin'. You're just a fast little nigger."

I jumped to my feet and into his face. He'd said the magic word.

"What did you just say?"

I stayed right in his face until the refs and my teammates pulled me away. He just stared back at me, smiling. My teammates finally got me back into the huddle. I kept staring at the linebacker while Josh called the play. I was okay with smack-talking. I loved talking smack myself, but saying that word like that, it crossed the line.

On second down, we tried one of our screen passes—a misdirection play where Josh fakes a handoff to me towards the right and then rolls out to the left, only to throw the ball all the way back to me across the field—and it worked. When I caught the ball, there were blockers out in front. I followed them down the right sideline and it wasn't until I reached the goal line that there was a defender. It was my good friend the linebacker. It was him against me. I put my helmet down and into his chest. He gasped a little as I bowled him over into the end zone. The referee raised two hands into the air. I stood up. My teammates mobbed me.

I looked down at the linebacker as he tried to catch his breath.

"Yeah, white boy," I said. "You better watch your mouth."

He tried to get up quickly, but didn't have enough air in his chest.

Twenty-one to twenty-one with one more quarter left in the season—one more quarter to settle the championship.

I ran to the sideline and Coach Watson gave me hug. He looked me in the eyes.

"What did he say?" he asked.

Part of me wanted to tell Coach Watson that the linebacker had said, but the other part didn't. I wasn't no snitch. Besides what could Coach Watson do? *I* was the one out there on the field. I could take care myself.

"Nothing," I said, "just some crap."

They got the ball and went to work on offense. We continued blitzing on almost every play and the results were mixed at best. On one play we'd get a little pressure and force an incompletion, and on the next they'd hit a fifteen-yard pass.

They gained five first downs and ate up more than half the fourth quarter. I couldn't help the team from the sidelines. Coach Watson wouldn't look at me because he knew I wanted to get in on defense. I had to do something, though. I couldn't let our defense go out like that.

They had third and eight from our twenty-five-yard line. There were four minutes to go in the game. They called a timeout and our defense ran over to the sideline. They were gassed—all of them—bending over, breathing hard, hands on knees. Coach didn't say anything at first. He just wanted them to catch their breath. I tried one last time to help out.

"Coach, please, let me get out there and rush the passer," I said. "The guys are tired."

"Marcus," he said. "I told you already, I need you on offense. I need you for the last drive."

"Then at least hear me out," I said. "Don't blitz.

Just play it straight up. You can't leave the corners out there on an island."

He thought for a second as he eyed the field. The refs were getting ready to blow the whistle to end the timeout.

"Okay," he said to the huddle. The guys tried their best to move their eyes and focus on what he had to say. "Fake the A-gap blitz. Then at the snap, back off into base cover-two."

Everyone in the huddle looked relieved.

"If they have twin receivers on one side, watch for the dig with the nine route going behind it," Coach said right before the ref blew the whistle.

Our guys ran back onto the field.

Coach turned to me. "I hope this works," he said. "With no pressure, their QB may just pick us apart. He got game."

"He's been doing it all game anyway, no matter what defense we play," I said. "Playing it this way might catch them off guard at least."

Coach nodded, spread his legs apart, and put his hands on his knees. He focused on the field.

Their QB scanned our defense before the play. Our middle linebacker, Reggie, stood right up in the A-gap, showing the blitz. The QB put his receiver in motion and got underneath the center. When he snapped the ball, Reggie dropped back into coverage and the QB hesitated as he kept back-pedaling, looking for a receiver to get open. But our zone defense worked. There were no openings for their receivers. The QB had to throw the ball out of bounds under heavy pressure from our D-line.

Fourth down.

Our sideline exploded with cheers.

They kept their offense out on the field and Coach Watson did the same with our defense.

He turned to me. "They're not gonna go for it here. They gotta try the field goal."

"I don't know," I said. "It's looks like they're gonna go for it."

Their QB broke the huddle, took the offense

to the line of scrimmage, and then stood back and eyed his coach. The coach sent hand signals in and it looked like they weren't on the same page. The QB looked confused and frustrated. Coach Watson had already signaled to Reggie that we were running the same defense as the play before, so we were set.

The QB was rattled; he got down underneath the center and right before snapping the ball, their coach ran onto the field to get the referee's attention for a timeout. The ref blew the whistle right before the snap and suddenly the whole stadium was quiet. Both teams ran to their sidelines. Coach Watson eyed the other sideline during the timeout while our defensive coordinator talked to the defense. He pushed his way into the huddle right before the timeout was over.

"Okay, listen up!" he said. "They're gonna kick. I saw their kicker getting warmed up and the coach just had a quick talk with him. Be alert for the fake! Don't jump off sides! Just make sure you follow the ball!"

The referee blew his whistle for the teams to get back on the field.

Coach Watson didn't break the huddle yet.

"There are three minutes and thirty seconds left to go in the game. Don't worry if they make the field goal. There's plenty of time for our offense to go down and score a touchdown to win the game."

He smiled and looked around the huddle. The guys in the huddle smiled back.

"Just be alert for the fake!" he repeated.

The ref blew the whistle again. Coach Watson was right; the other team was set up for the field goal. Their kicker was already in his spot two yards back from the holder.

"Watch the fake!" Coach Watson yelled again and again while pointing to his eyes.

The holder looked up to the kicker and the kicker nodded to him. The holder put his hand out and the center snapped the ball. The kicker took two small steps and kicked the ball as hard as he could. It went straight through the uprights and their sideline went crazy. The kicker pumped his fist and jumped into the arms of one of their huge lineman.

They were up twenty-four to twenty-one.

I knew we were going to win the game, though.

Coach Watson pulled Josh and me aside.

"We still have time to run the ball," he said. "But Josh, you have to make sure we hustle to the line in between plays. That clock is moving. Hurry, but don't rush."

"Aight," Josh said with a nod.

"It's your time," Coach Watson said to me. "It's your time, Marcus."

I looked straight into his eyes. He was right. It was my time.

We took over possession at our own twenty-eight-yard line. I glared at the linebacker as I ran out on the field. He stared right back at me without blinking.

Josh called the play in the huddle: a draw to the left. When we got to the line, I could see that their defense was out of place. If I could just hit the hole clean, we'd get a big gain.

Josh snapped the ball and took his drop like it was a pass play. At the last second, he handed the ball off to me and I looked up to find a huge hole to the left. I asked my legs for a burst of speed and they gave it to me. I got through the first wave of defenders and into their secondary. By the time one of their cornerbacks dragged me down, I was all the way out to their forty-five-yard line.

The clock was ticking, there were two minutes and thirty seconds to go, and we only had one timeout left. Josh looked over to the sideline to get the next play call. I looked at Coach Watson and he put both his hands out and pressed them flat down, telling us to "stay calm."

I felt calm. Josh quickly called the next play in the huddle. It was another running play. This time, Josh would fake a handoff to me to the right and keep it to the left. We got to the line again, and this time I saw that their defense was gassed. They were creeping up again to stop me. Josh snapped the ball and faked the handoff to me. Their whole defense flowed to the right and Josh had open field to the left. About ten yards past the line of scrimmage, he cut it back, and found the sideline. When a defender finally got close to him, he cut it back one more time, and found himself in the middle of the field. He was down to the fifteen-yard line when they tackled him. Our sideline exploded with excitement. I looked to their sideline and it was quiet. We could all feel how this was going to turn out. Everyone in that stadium knew that there was nothing they could do to stop us—nothing they could do to stop me.

The clock ticked down. There was only a minute and a half left. Josh was breathing hard and couldn't look up at the sideline to get the next play. Coach Watson put his hands out again.

"There's no rush!" he yelled. "Take your time!"

I pulled on Josh's jersey. "Come on, man," I said. "You good?"

He swallowed some air. He had his hands on hips. "Yeah," he said. "I'm good."

I looked up at the clock and there was a minute left. Josh finally got the play call. It was a toss sweep to the left. We took our time getting to the line because Josh needed every breath of air that he could get. He snapped the ball and pitched it to me. Their whole defense followed me, flowing to the left like a pack of wild dogs. I knew what I was going to do. I could see the play in my head before it happened on the field. I strung the run out all the way to the sideline. At the last second, I put my foot in the ground, cut back sharply, and ran as fast as I could toward the middle of the field. I could see the end zone getting closer. I thought about launching myself into the air for the score, but I was too far away. Three of their guys dragged me down at the five-yard line. I quickly got to my feet and looked up at the scoreboard. There were thirty seconds left and counting.

Coach Watson called our last timeout and we

jogged over to the sideline. Our fans were cheering us on, but still tense because the job wasn't done yet.

There weren't many words on the sidelines— no more speeches from Coach Watson, no more encouragement from teammates. We knew what we had to do. I knew what I had to do. Also, both teams knew exactly what was going to happen on the next play: I was going to get the ball. The only missing part was whether or not I was going to score. That was the only drama left.

With a few seconds to go in the timeout, Coach Watson stood in front us.

"It's okay if we don't get in on this play; there's time for one more after that," he said calmly. "If we don't get in, just look to me for the play call. And stay calm."

The ref blew his whistle to end the timeout.

"Go get it!" Coach said.

Josh gave us the play in the huddle. It was a power run to the right—ninety-two power—and it brought a smile to my face. I scored twenty touchdowns on that play during the season. Their defense was worn down. They weren't going to be able to stop it.

Our offense got set at the line. I couldn't hear the crowd at that point. I couldn't hear Josh call out the signals either. I couldn't hear anything. I focused my eyes on their linebacker who was talking smack to me. It was all in good fun, the smack-talking, until he'd said the magic word. If we were out on the streets and he did that, it would be trouble for him. But we were on the field. And the best way to shut him up would be to run him over and score the game-winning touchdown.

Josh snapped the ball and my legs fired. He handed me the ball and the hole was as big as day. I could've walked into the end zone. I hit the hole as hard as I could. I was inches away from the goal line when I got drilled on my right side. I didn't see it coming; he lit me up. The ball popped out of my right arm when the contact was made. It floated up in the black sky as I fell down to the turf. I reached up for the ball, but it was no use. It was too far out of my reach.

I was on my back looking up at the sky when I heard it. Their players kept screaming, "We got it! We got it! It's ours!" Then the ref yelled, "Blue ball!" And then their sideline erupted.

Game over.

I lost the game for us.

One of my teammates helped me up off the field and my head hung as soon as I got to my feet. I managed to look up at our sideline and there was a mixture of shock and sadness on people's faces. Coach Watson had both hands on his head with his mouth wide open. I dropped my head again, started to walk off the field, and kept it down until I ran into someone's huge body. It was the linebacker again. My first thought was that he'd squash the beef that was going on between us since the game was over. I was so shocked from my fumble, so weakened by it, that I had forgotten he called me a "nigger." My eyes were soft when I looked up at him. I was willing to give him respect because I knew how hard he played. But after one look at his face, I knew he wasn't there to squash it. His eyes taunted me. He grinned like he had stolen my milk money and there wasn't anything I could do about it.

"See?" he said. "You're nothin' but a hotshot nigger. When the game's on the line, you can't handle it. Go home to your screwed up part of town. I'm gonna go home to my big house with my trophy."

I lunged at him, gripped his facemask with one hand, and threw punches at his stomach with the other. He tried as hard as he could to slow me down—he was gritting his teeth and digging his cleats into the turf—but eventually I overpowered him and got him on his back. I got on top of him and ripped his helmet off. I threw as many punches at his face as I could before being crashed by a wave of people. Once again, I couldn't hear anything other than the word "nigger" repeated over and over in my head. All I saw was red.

A couple of my teammates tried to pull me away and a couple of his did the same. I broke free with a few wild swings of my elbows and saw Coach Watson out of the corner of my eye. The look on his face was terrible as he approached. It was a look of disappointment and fear.

I shrugged it off as I went after the linebacker again. He was on his feet, just breaking away from his teammates. His nose and mouth were painted in blood and it flowed fast onto his white jersey. For some reason, the grin was still on his face.

I ripped my helmet off and gave him a wild look. I threw my shoulder into his mid-section and tried to get him on the ground again. This time he stayed up, throwing sharp elbows into the back of my shoulder pads. I held on tight, pushing him all the way into the corner of the end zone until his back was right up against the barrier between the field and the stands. Players from each team were there too, either fighting or trying to stop fights. It was hard to get air. I could feel people digging their hands into me trying to rip me off of him, but I wouldn't let go. A few of our fans jumped down from the barrier and into the end zone. They started swinging wildly at the linebacker. I looked around at the chaos and suddenly my arms went dead. I let go of the linebacker and fell down to the ground. I stayed on my back and tried to look up at the black sky, but the mess of people fighting, screaming, and cursing was in the way. I closed my eyes and felt warm water sting them. This night was supposed to be special. It wasn't supposed to go down like that. I couldn't open my eyes to see the reality. I just focused on the burn instead.

SIX

The day after the fight was a blur. I didn't leave the house or talk with anybody. I expected to hear from Joe one way or another, but I never did. I didn't mind; my mom left me to myself all day. She went out clothes shopping like she always did on Sundays.

I ordered takeout at some point before it got dark. The only time I got out of bed was to pay the boy who brought me a sub with fries. Other than that, my Sunday was spent dropping in and out of sleep, hoping that I didn't waste my chance, that I didn't throw it all away.

I woke up early Monday morning and went to school. I knew the guys on the basketball team had a workout planned before first period. Even though I told Coach Jones that I needed a little break after the football season, I decided to attend the workout. I needed to get my mind off my situation.

When I entered the gym, the rest of the team was there getting changed and warmed up. Coach Jones wasn't present because it wasn't a mandatory workout. It was just a little thing the basketball team liked to do on their own before school early in the season.

I saw disbelief on most of the guys' faces. They probably weren't sure if I was allowed at school, let alone on the team. *I* wasn't sure either. I hadn't heard from Coach Watson, Coach Jones, or anyone else from school.

Errol, the starting point guard and best player

on the basketball team, walked over and shook my hand. He was the only one.

"What up, Marcus?" he said.

"What up, E?"

"Yo, what happened out there?" he asked. "One minute you're doin' your thing and the next"—he shook his head—"you're whalin' out on that big white boy."

I stared at Errol for a minute.

One half of my brain said that I needed to start defending myself—make it known that the white boy called me a "nigger" and get some support on my side—but the other half said that this was all a test. If playing sports didn't work out for me, I'd have to go out on the streets and handle my business like any other West Baltimore hustler. Over the years, it was easy to see that not being able to keep a secret was a weakness. If I learned anything growing up on the west side, anything at all, it was that a weakness could get you killed real quick.

"I don't know," I said. "It just . . . happened.

It was like I could see it happening before it even went down. And I couldn't do nothing to stop it."

"Damn," he said. "You hear from Coach Jones?"

"Nah," I said. "I just showed up. No one's said a word on it."

He nodded. "Cool. You wanna run with us?"

"Yeah. I need to get away from the drama while I can."

Errol and I shook hands again and I went to the sideline. I quietly changed into to my workout clothes while the other guys joked and laughed with each other.

We warmed up with the usual drills: layups, three-man weaves, three-on-twos. It felt good being around the guys. I didn't want to be alone with my thoughts and with nothing to do. I had to be around people. I had to do something. Sports were what I loved most—other than the west side—and I don't know what I would've done if the school decided to get rid of me. I stopped myself from thinking that.

I wasn't sore from the beating I took—on and off the field—during the championship game. My speed was where it usually was and my hops—one of my biggest weapons on the basketball court—were even higher than usual because my body was already primed for action.

When it wasn't my turn to take part in a drill, I watched the other guys as they went. Every guy on the team had his own style—some were flashy, some just kept it simple. A few liked to talk a lot while others didn't say a word. I hadn't looked at things that way before. I used to think that we all dealt with being from West Baltimore the same way, but there were different ways to handle yourself. I realized that then.

It was Errol's turn in the three-on-two drills. He was paired up on offense with two of the most athletic wings on the team. He led the break, dribbling straight down the middle of the court. He directed traffic with his eyes—a sign of a great point guard—and when the first defender committed too early, Errol made him pay. He looked off the second defender and hit one of his wings, striding down the left side with a sweet no-look pass that was finished with a nasty one-handed slam.

The guys went crazy. The gym was filled with hollers and taunts. It felt good to be out of the fire and in the mix again. I just wanted to enjoy it. I wasn't sure how much time I had left.

Errol was definitely the leader of this team. Like me on the football team, he led with both words and actions. He made the game look easy and that got your attention. Once he had it, he could move you with his words too.

We finished up with the drills and Errol called us all up to center court. We all ran to center court, circled up, and then looked up at him when he was ready to speak.

"We all know what happened the other night with Marcus," Errol said, looking around the circle. "And after it happened, we weren't sure if he was gonna be with us or not."

He paused and looked at me.

"But whatever happens, we're gonna have his back," he said.

The gym was silent.

"Because he's one of us," he said.

A few of the guys patted me on the back and I nodded to Errol in thanks. He didn't have to do that and it felt good. It felt good knowing that someone had my back.

"Let's get a little run in before school starts," Errol said with a smile. "I'll choose the teams."

I walked over to a dark corner of the gym to get a final stretch in before the pickup game. I took five deep breaths and then I was good. When I turned around, Errol was there.

"You're gonna run with my squad," he said.

"Cool," I said.

"Let's do this," he said.

In basketball, I went between the shooting guard and small forward positions, depending on which player Coach Jones needed me to guard on the other team. I never really settled on a position because defense was my strong suit. In football, you can pick one or two positions to play and just focus on those one or two jobs out on the field. I played running back, so my job was to get the ball in the end zone. Pretty simple. But basketball is different—you gotta be able to do a little bit of everything.

I could do that.

You also gotta work together with the other four guys on the court.

I could do that too.

On the first possession of the game, I ripped an offensive rebound down off a teammate's missed shot and found another teammate underneath the hoop for a layup. Errol tapped me on the back of the head as I ran down the floor. That was all I needed to get right back into it: one offensive rebound, one pass to a teammate. I was wrong before when I talked to Coach Jones. I didn't need any rest after the long football season. Being away from sports for one day was enough. I don't know how I'd react if they took it away for good.

I shot the gap on their first offensive possession and came up with the steal. I raced down the floor and rose up for a two-handed jam. I slapped the backboard and screamed when my feet hit the floor.

The other squad hit a three-pointer on their next possession and the score was four to three. Errol brought the ball up the court and called for me to come up and set a pick on his man. I did, and when Errol turned the corner, I rolled straight down the middle of the lane toward the hoop. He used his eyes again, looking off the defender in the paint, and threaded a one-handed bounce pass to me. I caught the ball through all the long-armed defenders, and went straight in for the layup.

Six to three, our way.

I sprinted to catch up with Errol, who was already back on defense.

"That's a sweet pass, Boy," I said.

"Good catch," he said with a nod and high five.

We exchanged buckets on the next few possessions and it wasn't until I made the play of the game that our side took control for good. The other squad got a steal and went the other way on a fast break. Instead of giving up on the play and letting them have an easy two points, Errol and I sprinted back on defense as fast as we could. Errol got down there first and elevated to challenge the layup attempt. Being away from the team for a while made me forget how high he could jump. Because the player had to go around Errol, I had enough time to come in for the block. I got a piece of the shot with the tip of my right index finger and the ball went straight into Errol's hands. He went the other way with it and I watched from where I was with my hands on my knees as he found one of our teammates for an open three-pointer. He knocked it down, and from that point, the game was ours.

Errol ran straight down the floor in my direction, and when I caught my breath, we both went into the air for a chest bump that brought thunder.

Basketball was beautiful like that. It could change on one little effort play. Just as fast as you're running down to score on one end, the other team could run the ball right back at you.

After that play, I was feeling good and sure of myself. I knew that the basketball court was where I belonged. I liked being out there with my teammates and I hoped that this wasn't my last time. I hoped that I'd get another chance.

The next time down, Errol stopped dribbling the ball right in the middle of the action. Something caught his glance behind me. I turned around and saw what it was. It was Coach Jones and he wasn't happy.

He walked onto the court straight over to me.

I knew what he wanted.

The gym was silent again. Everyone's eyes were on Coach Jones and me.

"You can't be out here, Marcus," he said. "You have to come with me. Mr. Watkins wants to see you in his office."

I nodded, but didn't say anything.

I walked over to the sideline to get my stuff. Errol ran over to me and patted me on the back.

"Whatever happens," he said.

I nodded and we shook one last time.

I followed Coach Jones out of the gym and into the hallway. School was mostly empty because there was still an hour before homeroom.

"Go take a quick a shower," he said, "and then meet me in my office. We'll walk over there together."

He was ahead of me in the hallway and I hurried to catch up with him.

"Any idea how this is going to go, Coach?" I asked.

He looked over at me with concern.

"No, Marcus." he said. "I haven't heard anything. Neither has Coach Watson. We'll all find out together."

SEVEN

"The superintendent of the city of Baltimore wants to have you expelled, Marcus," Assistant Principal Watkins said to me in his office. "Because of your history, and the ugliness of the events the other night, he wants you out of our city's schools."

I didn't reply. I just sat across from him, staring past him.

Coach Watson and Coach Jones were there too. My mom *was* in there as well, but when the meeting started, she got hysterical and started bawling. She had to be escorted out of the office.

"Do you know how serious this is, Marcus?" Mr. Watkins said, tilting his head to catch my eye.

I still didn't reply.

"If I could make a comment, Assistant Principal Watkins," Coach Watson said from behind me. "I know Marcus, sir. I know there have been some issues with anger and violence in his past. But he has been doing a lot better these past couple of years. There's been progress."

Mr. Watkins rolled his eyes. "How does Saturday night represent progress?"

"That was . . . " Coach Watson said. "There's no explanation for that. No excuse. But I know he didn't start it. That boy on the other team was digging at Marcus all game. Marcus knows how much he means to the team."

Coach Watson waved a hand over to Coach Jones. "Both of our teams," he said.

Coach Jones nodded.

"He wouldn't put himself and the whole team at risk in the state championship game," Coach Watson added. "Something went down on that field that Marcus isn't telling us about."

Mr. Watkins picked up *The Baltimore Sun* from his desk. He was reading the article that covered the championship game; the title of the article mentioned the brawl.

I slumped down in my chair.

"Here it says that Marcus was the instigator," Mr. Watkins said, tossing the newspaper back down on his desk. "And I called the principal from the school we played the other night. Their player swears that Marcus was the aggressor. And that young man's record is impeccable."

I rolled my eyes and turned to Coach Watson. He did the same.

"Well," Mr. Watkins said. "Do you have anything you want to add, Marcus?"

"Add?" I asked.

"Do you have anything that you want to say in your defense?" he asked.

"Now's the time, Son," Coach Watson said. "Tell us what happened out there."

I thought on it for a second, shook my head, and smiled.

"The only thing that I can say in my defense is that I ain't no snitch. Whatever happened the other night is done. I can't do nothing to change it. So I gotta carry it. Whatever it is."

I looked back to my two coaches. Coach Watson just stared at me and Coach Jones shook his head.

Mr. Watkins eyed me with no emotion on his face. "You're one lucky person, Marcus," he said.

Those words surprised me.

"It just so happens that the school superintendent is a good friend of one Joseph Milsap."

My eyes focused on Mr. Watkins's eyes.

"Do you know Mr. Milsap?"

"You mean *Joe*?" I asked.

"Probably *Joe* to you," he said, "but in the city of Baltimore, it's Joseph Milsap."

"So?" I asked.

"So, he's saved you," he said. "After talking with Mr. Milsap, the school superintendent decided to suspend you from school for a week with the hope that that will be enough time for the heat from Saturday night to cool down. You're also going to do some community service. We'll let you know where and when to get that all squared away."

I turned around and Coach Jones looked relieved. I was relieved.

Coach Watson still looked upset. I couldn't look him in the face.

"Of course, you won't be able to join the basketball team until your suspension from school is served," Mr. Watkins said.

"I understand," I said.

"Good," he said. "Use this time off to think about your life, Marcus. Think about your troubled past and think long and hard about Saturday night. This is your last chance. Make sure you don't flush it down the toilet."

I nodded.

"You're dismissed," he said.

Coach Watson said he'd give me a ride home after the meeting with Mr. Watkins. We walked to his car in the teachers' parking lot about ten minutes before homeroom and the chill was definitely in the air. I zipped up my jacket as high as it would go.

"Watkins is a jerk," Coach Watson said as he unlocked the car doors.

I didn't say anything to that. I just got into the passenger seat and shut the door.

"I think you're making a mistake, Marcus," he said. "It'd be better for you to come clean."

"You think so?" I asked.

"Yeah, this is different," he said. "This wouldn't be snitching. A snitch is somebody in the game. They talk to the authorities in order to get themselves out of trouble. I grew up on the same streets you did—I know why you're not talking. But in this case, it makes no sense."

"Seems like the same thing to me, Coach," I said.

"It's not."

We drove down Fayette and the corners were already back in business. I could see that the heat from Chris's murder was gone. Things were normal again in West Baltimore.

"Let's assume that you're right," I said. "I still don't want to form any habits, you know what I mean, Coach?"

"Habits?" he asked, looking at me uneasily.

"Yeah, I don't want to put it in my head that it's okay to talk to the authorities, no matter what the situation is," I said, unzipping my coat.

The heater was turned way up in Coach's car.

Coach Watson didn't say anything.

"You're from the same place I'm from," I said.

"That's right."

"Gotta keep it tight out here," I said. "No mistakes. Guys are watchin' out here. Watchin' your every move."

"I hear you," he said as he stopped his car in front of my apartment building. "But this is different. You gotta understand that. You're different than these other guys. The streets are out here. The game is out here. This thing that happened the other night at the championship game, it's your life. The two things ain't connected."

"I don't know, Coach," I said. "They feel connected."

"You wanna play in the NFL or the NBA? You wanna go to college?" He asked.

"You know I do," I said.

"Then you need to leave the streets behind you, Marcus. You need to look ahead. In that world, the rules on the street ain't the rules you play by."

I shook Coach Watson's hand and got out of his car. He didn't pull away from the curb right away. He was waiting for me to respond.

I didn't say a word back to him, though. I just zipped up my coat again and kept walking all the way to the front door of my apartment building.

EIGHT

My mom was out for the night. I didn't do much of anything during the first day of my suspension from school. I didn't answer any calls at the house—most of them would be from reporters, Coach Watson warned—and I didn't go outside. I just watched TV all day and took a bunch of naps. It felt good to just chill. I didn't have much time during the school year to do that. I was always running to practice and games. One day on the field, another on the court. Maybe I needed a little time off to get my head right.

I called around town looking for Joe again, but he was nowhere to be found. I was surprised to find out that he wasn't at the championship game and even more surprised that he didn't reach out to me after the brawl. I also wanted to thank him for saving me. Again. If it wasn't for him, Mr. Watkins and the school superintendent would've gladly thrown me out of school. Then I'd be out on those corners.

Around eight o'clock that night there was a knock at my door. I wasn't expecting anybody. My first thought was that I'd open the door and see Joe, or at least one of his associates who'd either give me a message from him or take me to meet him.

But it wasn't Joe.

It was Byron. He stood in my doorway wearing a black hoodie, black Dickies, complete with black Timberlands. He eyed me without blinking. My eyes must've been pretty surprised.

"You gonna invite me in, man?" he asked.

I moved out of the way and he entered. He looked around the living room and nodded his head in confirmation.

"Damn," he said. "This is nice. Joe got you livin' the fast life."

"Nah, this ain't fast," I said. "It's just a little something."

I waved him over to the couches and we sat down. I turned the TV off and we stared at each other for a minute.

"What's up?" I finally asked.

"I heard about the other night at the game," he said. "Read about it in the Sun."

"You didn't come to the game?" I asked. "I left you and them other guys some tickets at will-call."

"Nah," he said. "Mel, Petey, and Little Rick went. They said that you balled out until you lost your mind."

He chuckled.

"They jumped onto the field during the fight, got a few little punches in," he said.

"That was crazy," I said.

"I was taking care of something else, that night," he said. "I did some investigating."

"Of?"

"Chris."

I sat up straight and leaned back against the spine of the couch.

"What's up?"

"Joe's nowhere to be found."

I thought about my own troubles getting hold of Joe and my eyes narrowed.

"I didn't even take my last re-up from Joe," he said. "I took it from some East Side guy named Mike-Mike. Told me Joe would reach out soon— whatever that means."

I thought it was weird, but shook it off quickly.

"Maybe Joe is just layin' low right now," I said. "Let things cool off a little."

Byron shook his head slowly.

"Joe always stays on top of re-ups, even when the cops is on him," he said. "I didn't even hear from Joe or one of his people about taking the re-up from East Side."

"What are you thinking?"

"Joe's up into something," he said with sureness in his voice. "He killed Chris. Like I said the other day."

"So you think the fact that he's hiding right now means that he killed Chris?"

"Hell yeah."

"I told you the other day, Joe wouldn't do Chris like that."

"I thought you said that he told you that Chris was snitching."

"Yeah," I said, caught off guard by Byron's strong memory. "But Joe would tell me if he had to do Chris. Joe doesn't answer to anybody, let alone me."

Byron stared at me the whole time as I talked. His eyes met mine and didn't blink.

"If Chris was snitching and Joe had to kill him, I would find out," I said. "Joe would tell me."

"You sure about that?" he asked.

"Yeah."

"And has Joe reached out to you in these past few days?" he asked. "I mean, Chris's body is damn near ice cold and if you're as tight as you say you are with Joe, he would have told you by now that he was the one who did Chris."

"Well, no, I haven't heard from him lately," I said weakly. "But that's my point, man. Joe told me that Chris was snitching and that's why he got dead. He didn't say nothin' about being responsible for it."

"And you're good with that?" he asked, eying me again.

"I trust Joe," I said.

I felt doubt in those words as I said them. I'm sure Byron recognized that. We went back far enough that he knew when I meant something and also when I didn't. And Joe—with all he had done for my mom and me—was a businessman. If anything threatened that business, whether it was snitching or something else, he'd take care of it quick.

"Nah," Byron said, shaking his head. "You want to know the truth just like I do."

I didn't say anything to that.

"So let's find out the truth," he said.

"What do you mean?" I asked. "How?"

"Let's find out if Chris was really snitching."

"How?"

"Come out on the streets with me and I'll show you," he said. "I know you got some time off from school and basketball. You ain't got nothin' else to do."

I stood up from the couch and he did the same. I started walking over to the front door of the apartment. Byron followed me.

"We gotta do this for Chris," he said, putting his hand on my back.

I turned around to face him.

"And what if we find out that Chris wasn't snitching and that Joe killed him. Then what?" I asked.

Byron flashed the smile that I remembered from when we were kids.

"Like I said the other day out on my corner," he said, "if Joe is responsible, he has to get got. That oldhead guy has been the king of the west side too long anyhow."

"Crap," I said. "King of Baltimore."

He nodded along to that as he walked past me and turned the knob to open the door.

"You're gonna need proof to do what you're saying, B," I said to his back. "And not just a little proof. You're gonna need a big, fat mess of proof."

He turned around and eyed me one last time. His eyes were soft this time and they finally looked like the eyes of an old friend.

"Here's a little bit of proof for you, Marcus," he said. "I found it on the streets this past weekend during my little investigation."

I crossed my arms and waited for it.

"Joe killed you and Chris's friendship," he said. "I mean, think on it, you two didn't have any beefs over the years, no drama. It just stopped all of sudden."

He was right; there was nothing that happened between Chris and me to end our friendship. Up until then, I thought that we had just grown apart.

"Joe did that," he said. "You think on it tonight."

I stood there staring at him.

"Come out on the streets with me, Marcus," he said. "It's been too long. If not for me, then for Chris."

He turned around and walked out the door.

I waited for a second and then slowly followed him out. The truth was, I really didn't want to go outside into the cold. I didn't want to put myself at more risk. But I also didn't want to disrespect my boy Chris. In any case, by the time I turned my head and looked down the hallway, Byron was gone. He was on his way back out into the cold, cold streets, leaving me behind in the heat.

NINE

I called Byron early the next morning to tell him I was up. He said that he knew I wouldn't let him down. He wanted me to meet him somewhere downtown near the Harbor Place. I didn't know the place. He gave me an address and said to meet him at eleven.

Still no word from Joe. I was starting to think that Byron was on to something, and that spark of curiosity was enough for me to want to know more. I ate some cereal, took a shower, and changed into a pair of black jeans, black Timberlands, and a black hoodie. I looked out the window and saw a gray-covered sky. I grabbed a black beanie and left my apartment.

When I hit the pavement, the temperature was warmer than the day before and the air was moist like it was about to rain. I wished that the weather would just make up its mind.

I had to decide how I was going to get downtown. It was too far to walk, so that was out. Usually, I'd call one of Joe's people if I needed a ride, but now wasn't a good time for that. There was also the bus, but I hadn't been on a Baltimore city bus since I was kid and wasn't about to start riding them again.

I chose the last option that was available—a method of transportation unique to Baltimore.

I walked to the corner of Lexington and Fayette and then stopped. I threw two fingers in the air and waited for a pop-up taxi to stop. The number of fingers you threw in the air told the drivers how many miles you were going. The price you paid to the driver was based on miles driven. From what I knew, downtown was about two miles away from my neighborhood on the west side. I took my beanie off as I waited for a car to stop. The air was too thick for a hat like that; I started to sweat.

After two minutes with my hand up, an old, brown mess of a station wagon pulled over next to me. He left his engine running and stood up from the driver's seat, poking the top half of his body out of the driver side window and over the roof of the car.

"Two?" he asked.

I nodded. "I need to get downtown."

"That's at least three," he said.

"Nah, man, downtown Baltimore is two miles away from West Side."

He thought for a second.

"Aight," he said. "Get in."

I got into the backseat and gave him the address.

———

I was thirty minutes early when the driver dropped me off at the address. The spot looked like a bar—the kind of bar that was open early in the morning and didn't have a name. I stood across from it leaning on the side of a brick building and watching for any action. There was only a little. A couple of guys walked into the bar and one guy walked out. Two of them were white and one was black. I thought I recognized one of the white guys as a knocko who banged the corners in my neck of the woods.

Other than that, it was quiet in that part of town. The bar was just far enough from the harbor that there weren't any tourists. This looked like a local Baltimore bar. It looked like a cop bar. It made sense, too. Other than low-bottom alcoholics, the only other people in Baltimore who drank in the morning were cops.

I checked my watch and it was almost eleven. A black guy I recognized from the west side walked into the bar. Byron showed up right after that. He stood in front of the bar and looked out from his spot. I called over to him from across the street and he smiled, nodded, and pointed at me. He checked for cars and ran across the street.

"What up, my dude?" he said and we shook hands.

"This is a cop bar, ain't it?" I asked with a smile.

"How can you tell?"

"Easy."

He lit a Newport and blew the smoke away from me.

"What are we doing at a cop bar, B?" I asked.

"See about Chris," he said.

He headed back across the street to the bar and I followed him. He took two quick drags off his Newport before tossing it. He opened the door to the bar and held it for me.

When we walked in, the bar was dark and the air was still. Everything looked like it was made of the same type of old wood. The smell of stale beer and cigarettes stung my nose and made it twitch.

There were five people drinking at the wooden bar and one bartender. They were all older white guys. They stared at Byron and me for a moment, then went back to their beers.

Byron looked around the spot and saw his guy sitting at a circular booth in the back. He was the only other black person in the bar. It was the guy I saw enter the bar from across the street.

"You made it," he said to Byron, and they shook hands. He had a beer in front him—a Heineken— and a soft pack of Newports with a book of matches stacked on it.

He nodded to me.

I didn't know him personally, but I knew his face.

"What's up Marcus?" he said.

I nodded.

"Damn shame how that game ended the other night," he said, shaking his head. "You played like a beast."

"You were there?" I asked.

"I like to follow the stars coming out of B-More,"

he said. "Especially the ones that come out of West Side."

We sat down at the booth; Byron sat between him and me.

"Can I get you two anything?" he asked. "What's your taste?"

"Let me get a Crown Royal," Byron said with excitement in his eyes.

The man laughed a little, showing his teeth. "You can't drink no Crown Royal in the morning. You got to start slow with a beer. A light beer at that."

Byron slouched a little in the booth, looking hurt.

"I'll get you a Heineken," the man said, standing up from the booth. "I gotta school you young'uns."

He looked to me.

"How about you, Marcus?"

"I'm good," I said.

"That's smart. Athletes need to keep the body clean." He nodded and walked over to the bar.

I eyed him as he ordered. Joe always told me not to use drugs or alcohol. It was actually the first thing he ever told me when I was kid. And since that time, I never witnessed Joe drink or use drugs. He didn't even smoke cigarettes, even though most of the fools around the way smoked those Newports. He said that a man who used drugs and alcohol was weak. I took it to heart too. I followed in his footsteps, never taking a sip of beer, a hit from a joint, or a bump of cocaine.

The man returned with two more beers, one for Byron and another for himself.

"So," he said, sliding back into the booth.

"What did you call us all the way out here for?" I asked. "I mean, we're all from West Side. We could of done this back across Washington Boulevard."

The man smiled and looked to Byron.

"I see that I need to school you to these here rules of the game, Marcus," he said.

I wasn't smiling.

"This place here is safe," he said. "Ain't no West

Side guys up in here. You get a few hard stares from those white cops up there."

He nodded over to the bar up front.

"But there's no danger," he said. "We can talk in peace."

"Well talk!" I shot back.

Byron looked over to me and the look said that he needed me to cool out. There was also some surprise in his look—surprise that I had taken control of a meeting that he had set up.

"Okay," the man said. "First of all, why are you here? I know why Byron is here. But you, I'm not so sure."

"Me and Chris went back a ways," I said. "I'm trying to see if there's a good reason that he was killed."

"There's always a good reason," the man said, "for the person who's doin' the killing."

Byron jumped in. "What you got for us, Charles?"

When I was a kid, there was a man named

"Charlie" around the way. I recognized that this was him. He used to run with Joe at the beginning when Joe took control of a few important corners, but Charles didn't run with Joe anymore.

"Joe's getting sloppy," Charles said. "He's buying up all these guns, getting ready for a war that doesn't need to happen."

"A war?" I asked.

"Yeah," Charles said. "He already holds the power because he's the main distributor of dope and coke in this city. You can't sling drugs or get high in this town without Joe's fingerprints being all over it."

I already knew all that. He wasn't shedding any new light on anything for me. Byron knew all this too.

"What does that have to do with Chris getting killed?" I asked.

"*Everything*," he said. "You know that other boy, Peanut? He runs with that mob on Paca street?

Well he got dead a couple of weeks back. Same way your boy did."

"I heard about Peanut getting killed," Byron said. "But what you're saying, it don't make sense."

"Yeah," I said. "What's the connection?"

"Joe's trying to take over the whole city," Charles said. "He already owns the west side, and when it comes to drugs, that pretty much means you run Baltimore. But that ain't enough for Joe. He wants control of East Side too."

I looked at Byron and it still wasn't making enough sense. Not enough to believe him.

"Now think about it," Charles said. "There's always been a West Side drug trade and an East Side drug trade. The players in this city have always respected that. But Joe is going past that. He wants to change things."

"And where do *you* fit in this?" I asked.

"Me?" he asked with a grin. "I'm just an East Side player tryin' to get by."

"But you used to be West Side, right? I asked,

betting on my memory. "I remember you. You used to be with Joe. You knew my pops too."

"I'm surprised you remember me, Marcus," he said. "That was a long time ago. I remember you too, when you were just a little shorty. I knew your daddy well."

"You still ain't tell us about Chris," Byron said.

"Right," Charles said. "Well, your boy Chris and the other boy Peanut, they were like bait for the war that Joe is starting up."

"Bait?" Byron asked.

"Joe is going around killing his own people, then sayin' that they were snitchin'," he said.

I thought of the morning after Chris died, sitting there with Joe.

"But then he's also gonna put it out there that it's East Side people killing West Side people," he said. "And there's your war. Just add water."

Charles laughed at his own joke and took a deep pull off his beer.

"What you mean?" Byron asked. "He's gonna put mixed messages out there on the street?"

"Confusion," Charles said. "You get everybody all crazy with accusations and payback and all of a sudden no one knows why they're fighting or what they're fighting for."

He took another sip of his beer.

"But the most important thing for Joe is that there *is* fighting out on the streets," he added.

"How did you leave Joe?" I asked. "Usually, the only way out is a bullet in the dome."

"Me and Joe go way back," he said. "We came to an agreement."

I leaned back in the booth and eyed Charles. I didn't like him. He was a slimy guy.

"And I bet you'd be just fine if we," I pointed to Byron, "took Joe out. That would make your day, right?"

"The way Joe did your boy was foul," he said.

"But how do we know you ain't playing us?" I asked.

Now it was Charles's turn to eye me. He finished his second beer, licked his lips, and then wiped his mouth with his sleeve. I could see a little wildness in his eyes—you don't last too long slinging in Baltimore without it.

"My information is correct," he said, eying me. His eyes didn't blink when he spoke. "But I'll go you guys one further. I know a fiend who was on Mount and Fayette the night your boy fell."

Byron and I looked at each other and then back at Charles.

"I'll tell you where to find him and you can hear it from him," Charles said. "It was Joe's people, his closest people, that killed Chris that night."

Charles shook a Newport loose from his soft pack and put it behind his ear. He got up from the booth and shook his coat out. He put it on and looked down to us. He walked over to the bar and asked for a slip of paper and pen. He wrote something down on the paper and handed the pen back to the bartender. He walked back over to the booth and handed the slip of paper to me. There was a West Side address and name on it. I didn't recognize either of them.

"How you know about this?" I asked. "About the fiend seeing Chris killed?"

"Joe's getting sloppy," he said. "And I'm keeping thing tight."

Charles nodded to Byron and me, and left the bar. We watched the door for a few seconds after he walked out.

TEN

"Where you find that guy?" I asked Byron.

We were standing outside of the bar, across the street in front of the brick building. Byron had sparked another Newport and was drawing on it deeply.

"People like him ain't hard to find, man," he said.

"He just wants Joe out of the picture," I said. "He got too much to gain in all this. I don't trust him. He sees that you're mad about Chris and he's just feeding you this crap. He doesn't want to do the dirty work himself. Joe is a hard man to get to. Charles knows that better than anyone. But he sees you, a guy that runs one of Joe's corners, and he sees a chance. Charles can't get to Joe. With you being one Joe's crew chiefs, there's a slight chance *you* can."

"I hear you, man," Byron said, ashing his Newport on the sidewalk. "I know that he wants Joe to fall and that's why he's helping us. I know all that. But if Joe killed Chris and it ends up helping Charles, who cares? I mean, we agreed, if Chris wasn't snitching—"

"Talking to some fiend ain't gonna prove if Chris was snitching or not," I said loudly. "Let's say he tells us what Charles told us, that Joe's right-hand people did Chris. What does that prove? Joe's people could've gotten at Chris for snitching. And you know when someone has to fall, Joe sends his closest people."

Byron took a long drag off his Newport and it burned all the way down to the filter. He tossed it and then looked to me. He thought for a second.

"Joe is foul," he said.

"He is the most feared and respected player in this city," I said. "You don't think I know that he's foul? You can't get to where he is without being foul."

"I'm not talking about being hard, Marcus. That's not it," he said. "It goes past that."

"Well spit it out, man!" I said.

"Remember what I told you yesterday? About Joe putting an end to you and Chris's friendship?"

"Yeah."

"A few years ago, when you started getting really good at sports, Chris was really just getting started out on the corners."

"So?"

"And that's around the same time that you and Chris stopped hanging out."

"Yeah?"

"Joe went to Chris and told him to stay away from you. He told him that he didn't want anybody messin' with your chance to go pro. That some project guy like Chris had no business being around someone like you. Someone who was on his way out of here."

He paused for a second and then looked me right in the eyes, letting it sink in.

"That's why Chris stopped coming around you," he added. "Stopped calling you and stuff."

It hit me right in the teeth. I felt a tightness in my head behind my eyes. Byron had called things just like they happened. There never was a beef between Chris and me. We were tight one day and then the next day we weren't. I got busy with sports and he got busy with the corner. Life goes on, right? I never thought about what it all meant, but what Byron said was on point.

"Did Joe ever have that same talk with you?" I asked, almost out of breath.

Byron shook his head. "You and me stopped kicking it before you and Chris did. Remember?"

I nodded. Byron had a good memory of the past. I did too.

"Joe doesn't know that you and me were tight,"

he said. "But he does know that you and Chris were."

He stopped talking for a second as a black father and son passed us on the sidewalk.

"But I remember that we used to be tight, Marcus," he said in a lower voice. "Don't you?"

I nodded.

"I need to know something, B," I said. "How did you get in touch with Charles? Did he find you or the other way around?"

Byron didn't say anything. He just eyed me. I got up in his face.

"It's important!" I said. "Charles could be playing us! He could be on his way to Joe right now, telling him all this! And then guess what? While we think we're huntin' Joe, he's huntin' us! And you don't want that, man. I definitely don't want that!"

I was right up close to Byron's face with the collar of his shirt balled up in my left hand. My right hand was held in a fist. Byron was skinny compared to me and I could sense a little fear in his eyes and in his bones.

"Yo, cool out, man," he said in a tentative voice. "I should've known from the newspaper that you still got your temper. But I see it up close now. You always did know how to blow up on a guy."

"My bad," I said, backing up and giving him some space. I thought of the white linebacker from the championship game and quickly shook the thought of him out of my mind.

"I've been careful," he said quietly, as if Joe was right there listening in on us. "I haven't been talking to anyone who is connected to Joe. No one that could report back to Joe. Nobody except for you."

"So how'd you find this clown Charles?"

"You gotta wait on that, Marcus," he said. "You gotta trust me."

I looked at Byron and tried to see if he was playing me. That was another thing that Joe taught me at a young age. He taught me to look for the signs in a guy that was trying to run game. I couldn't see the signs on Byron. All I saw was pain—the pain of loss.

"Aight," I said. "Let's go see that fiend. If we can even find the guy."

Byron smiled and we shook on it.

"We gotta find out if Chris was snitching or not," I said. "I'll go all the way with you, if . . . "

We were both silent for a minute as we walked away from the bar.

Byron smiled. "You're already all the way in, Marcus," he said. "You just don't know it yet."

He stopped and looked out to the street, then walked to the edge of the sidewalk to catch us a real cab back to the west side. One stopped and Byron opened the rear door on the right. He turned back to me before getting in.

"But you're right," he said. "We gotta find out the truth. If not for Chris, then for ourselves."

He got into the cab and I followed him. We went back to the west side.

We didn't talk on the cab ride back across town. I looked out my window and Byron looked out of his.

Growing up, people in my neighborhood knew me because of my temper. I always had one and it was always big. My mom said that I got it from my father, but I wasn't sure. I didn't spend enough time around him to find out.

My temper got me in a lot of trouble growing up. I used to fight at school, on the football field, and on the basketball court at the drop of a hat. It could have been a look that someone gave me or just a single word. It didn't matter. I had to show the people around me that I was hard and fighting was the only way I knew how to do it.

Joe was the opposite. He was cool as could be. I never saw him lose his cool, even though he was having guys killed. I felt safe around Joe. He calmed me down.

When he started playing a big role in my life, helping my mama out after my dad was sent up to Jessup, he sat me down for a talk one day. I remembered it was a Saturday after one of my MTS Terps football games. I was in the seventh grade. He told me that I couldn't keep going about my business like I was. He said that the fighting had to stop or else my life would be short. I didn't get it at first. I didn't know any other way to get rid of my anger. But Joe kept talking to me and kept looking out for me, telling me I was doing a good job in sports and with my temper.

After a while, I started getting in fewer fights, and soon I wasn't fighting at all. The truth was, Joe had always been looking out for me. Even in telling Chris to stop talking with me—it was messed up, but I could see why he did it.

The brawl during the state championship game was my first involvement in a fight in more than two years. And the thing of it was, I wasn't even looking for a fight that night. I was trying my hardest to help my team win. That white boy on the other team just kept pushing me.

Byron looked across the backseat of the cab at me.

"What you thinking on?" he asked.

"Nothing," I said. "Nothing at all."

That wasn't the truth. I wondered what Joe had thought when he heard about the fight from the game. I really wondered why I hadn't heard from him yet and why he wasn't at the game. I tried to quickly figure out how it all pieced together and where my boy Chris fell into it.

———

The cab driver dropped us off at the address that Charles had handed to us. I didn't know that part of the west side well. It was the part with all of the scrap metal yards. There weren't many houses over there. The air was foul; it smelled like chemicals.

The only thing I knew about that part of the

west side was that a lot of fiends hung out around there and that meant you'd find a lot of shooting galleries as well.

We stood outside of an old one-story warehouse that looked like it was abandoned. We tried going through the front door but it was rusted shut. To the side of the building, there was a fence that lined all the way around to the back of the building. The lock on the fence was busted open. That's how the drug fiends were getting in.

"What if he's not in there?" I asked. "We're gonna walk into to a shooting gallery in the middle of all the dope fiends getting high and ask, 'Oh, is there some guy named Milt in here? We need to speak to him'?"

Byron found that funny. I didn't.

He walked through the opening in the fence and I followed.

There was a parking lot on the other side of the fence with no cars in it, just tents and old trashcans with burned wood and trash. I couldn't tell if there was anyone living in any of those tents, but I hoped that we didn't have to go looking for Milt in any of them. It smelled like piss back there mixed with the chemical smell that surrounded us. We held our noses as we made our way to the back entrance of the warehouse.

The rusted door whined as Byron pulled it open. The light from outdoors spilled into the dark space of the warehouse. No one inside moved or said anything when we opened the door. We weren't even sure that there was anyone inside.

We stood at the doorway looking in, waiting to see who was going to take the first step.

"You goin' in, man?" I asked.

He looked at me. "You first," he said.

"Come on," I said and walked in.

The smell was the first thing that hit. It smelled worse than the back parking lot. It was more intense, and even if you held your nose, the smell still crept in. As we carefully walked through the shooting gallery, we could start to see some of the fiends moving slowly in the darkness. I couldn't see any of their eyes, but could feel their stares on me. I made sure that Byron stayed close. I didn't want to lose him in there and I'm sure he felt the same way. We passed by one fiend who was knocked out. He was in a nod with his back leaning against the wall and the lower part of his body in a half-zipped sleeping bag. He still had the needle in his arm. We saw a few flames spark around the space and then heard the stuff cooking. I stopped and Byron bumped into my back.

"Well?" I asked.

"Well, what?"

"We don't know what he looks like," I said. "We gotta call out the name."

"You do it."

"I'm not doing it," I said. "You're the player. You do it."

Byron took a deep gulp of air. He had this look on his face that his skin was crawling just from being in there.

"Listen up!" he said. "I'm lookin' for a guy named Milt! Anybody points me out to the man, there's five in it for them!"

We heard the movements of the fiends, but no words. We heard a spoon hit the concrete floor and a glass bottle tip over.

"Make it ten!" Byron called out.

"Hey!" a voice said from the other side of the warehouse. We couldn't see who it was. We looked at each other and followed the sound of another "Hey!"

The man had his hand raised in the air when we got over to him. He stood up. He had ripped jeans and a wrinkled button-down shirt on. He was emaciated and his smell was sharp.

"You Milt?" I asked.

"That's me," he replied. "How can I help you?"

"You think we could go outside," Byron said, "and talk?"

"If you got business, Young Buck, we gonna have to take care of it here," he said.

We got closer to him so we wouldn't have to yell. I could see Byron's eyes lock in on him. There was hate in his eyes.

"We got your name from Charles," I said. "Do you know who I'm talking about?"

"Well that depends," he said. "Bust out that ten spot first and then we'll talk."

Byron jumped at him and grabbed at the back of his waistband. Next thing I knew, he had his nine in Milt's face. He pulled the hammer back and took a strong hold of his collar.

"Man, why don't you stop wastin' my time? I'll let this do my talking for me," Byron said.

Milt closed his eyes and his body went limp. Byron tried holding him up, but it was no use. The whole scene was pathetic. I grabbed Byron's shoulder with one arm and pulled him away from the fiend. He let go of Milt's collar.

"Come on, " I said. "You did call out that you are puttin' a ten up."

Byron looked at me and then fixed the hammer

back into its safe position. He put his whistle back into his waistband and went into his pocket to peel a ten off his roll. He tossed it at Milt, who was down on the floor in his sleeping bag with his face in his hands.

"Come on, Milt," I said. "We just want to talk. We don't want to hurt you."

Byron rolled his eyes.

Milt slowly stood back up—still in his sleeping bag—and his eyes were a little wet.

"One of you wouldn't happen to have a jack, would you?" he asked.

I looked to Byron with a raised eyebrow and he looked like he was going to explode. He pulled a cigarette from his pack and handed it to Milt.

"You need a light too?" Byron asked angrily.

"Nah, I'm cool," he said, reaching down to his sleeping bag and coming up with a pack of matches. He lit his cigarette and faced us again.

"Enough of this," Byron said. "We got some questions for you."

"Shoot," Milt said.

"How do you know Charles?" I asked.

Milt chuckled to himself. "What dope fiend doesn't know Charles?"

"You're West Side though, right?" I asked. "Charles slings on the east side."

"When you're a dope fiend, Young Buck, it don't matter where you're from. You chase the next blast wherever you can get it."

"Charles says you was out there the night a boy named Chris got killed on Mount and Fayette," Byron said. "A few nights ago?"

Milt nodded thoughtfully as he took a drag of the Newport. "Yeah. Yeah. Young kid, running the corner at night. If I'm not mistaken, it's your corner during the day."

He pointed a finger at Byron. I thought Byron was going to pull his gun on Milt again. I put an arm out in front of Byron just to protect Milt.

"I remember," Milt said. "Boy was shot at close range. One to the back of the head."

"Did you see who did it?" I asked.

"Big guy, dark," Milt said. "They pulled up in a black truck."

The black Expedition.

"Did he have dreads?" I asked. "The big guy who killed Chris?"

Milt nodded.

That sounded like Sheik, Joe's number two. He handled all of Joe's serious muscle work.

"And?" I asked.

"Couple guys get out of the driver side. Big guy gets out of the passenger side. They all walk over to Chris," he said. "There wasn't no drama at first. Just talk. Then all of sudden, the one standing behind, the big one with dreads, pulls out his gun and shoots that boy dead. It came out of nowhere."

And Sheik *never* drove. Sheik always rode shotgun.

I looked over to Byron and I'm sure he knew it too.

"And where were *you*?" Byron asked.

"I was in the alley 'round the corner," he said. "I'd just copped a vial from your boy."

Milt was moving around uncomfortably. He was getting restless standing there talking to us.

"One more question," I said. "What car were they driving?"

"I said a black truck."

"What kind of truck?"

"One of them SUVs," Milt said. "One of them Expeditions."

I looked over to Byron and if he didn't know before, he definitely knew now.

"Aight, Milt." I said. "Thanks."

Byron and I started to leave and Milt ran out in front of us.

"Seeing as I just helped you two, I was wondering if . . . "

He looked to Byron.

Byron sighed and shook his head. He turned around and got down on one knee. He took a little baggie out of his sock, picked a vial out of it, and put it between two fingers. He put the baggie back into his sock and stood back up.

He handed the vial to Milt. The vile had a red top. Milt took it in his hands like it was treasure and bowed his head to Byron. He hustled back to his sleeping bag, sat down in it, and zipped it back up. We walked away from Milt, and after a few steps, I couldn't help myself. I turned around to get one, last look at Milt, but it was too dark in there to see him anymore.

I turned back around, caught up with Byron, and we walked out of the warehouse and into the back parking lot. We held our noses again until we walked a few blocks away from the warehouse. It was good to get fresh air again.

Now we knew Joe was involved in Chris's death. Joe didn't say anything about that the morning after. All he said was that Chris was snitching and left it at that. The next thing we had to do was find out if Chris was really snitching. I didn't know what or who to believe anymore. I didn't know where this was going to take us next, but I definitely felt something that gave me a feeling that I rarely ever had: fear.

ELEVEN

Marcus walked with me back to my apartment. The weather was still way too nice for that time of year, giving an extra weird feeling to a day that was already plenty weird. I was sweating underneath my hoodie and couldn't wait to get to my apartment and chill. It was around three o'clock in the afternoon.

We didn't walk anywhere near school. We took the back streets because I didn't want to be seen by any friends, coaches, or teachers. I also didn't want to run into Joe or anyone from his circle. For all I knew, he'd be looking for us by now.

"What next?" I asked out in front of my building.

"You know Joe did it," Byron said, smoking a Newport.

"Yeah," I said. "There's just that one piece left."

He nodded while smoke crept out of his mouth. "We can do that tonight if you're up for it."

"Not tonight," I said.

"Aight," he said.

"Wanna tell me how we're gonna find out that Chris wasn't a snitch?"

"I can't," he said, stamping out his cigarette.

"What you mean?" I asked.

"I just can't say yet."

"You need to tell me!" I said. "I'm risking my life running all around town asking questions about Joe!"

He got right up into my face.

"Man, you think you're the only person risking your life?" he asked.

I could smell the cigarettes on his breath. He was *that* close. Face to face, our eyes were locked. Neither of us wanted to blink first.

It wasn't easy to trust people growing up where we did. I didn't trust many people, if any at all. Byron was the same. But I didn't see any lies written on his face. All I saw was the pain in his eyes.

"My bad," I said. "I didn't mean to get all up on you."

He calmed too. His body relaxed and he took a couple steps back. He lit another Newport and took a nervous drag.

"I understand where you're at," he said. "You got more to lose than a guy like me. I just thought you should know. Chris was always like a brother to me, and even though you two lost touch over the years, I'm sure it was the same for you too."

I nodded. A sick feeling formed in the pit of my stomach and it quickly turned into a slow, warm pain. I realized that I hadn't eaten since my bowl of cereal that morning, but the thought of food made me want to throw up.

"You aight?" he asked. "You look like you're about to spit up."

"I'm good," I said.

"Like I was saying," he said, "some things are bigger than money and these corners. And screw Joe, with his crown and his war. There are rules to this game. You don't kill a guy for no reason at all."

The pain was shooting from my toes to my head. I wobbled a little and Byron noticed it. He put a hand on my shoulder to keep me upright. I put my head down to try to calm myself. I took five deep breaths. I lifted my head back up to get air and the pain slowly went away. Byron took his hand off my shoulder. I side-stepped and couldn't catch my balance right away, but it slowly came back too.

Byron stood there just staring at me. He smoked his Newport to the filter and tossed the butt.

I closed my eyes and tried to slow my heart down.

"Yo," he said. "What's up?"

I caught my breath and looked over to him with a little wetness in my eyes.

"I'm fine," I said. "I'm good now."

"If you don't wanna go all the way, I understand," he said. "It means a lot to me that you've gone this far. I'll never forget that."

We shook hands.

"I can handle it the rest of the way," he said.

"If we find out that Chris wasn't a snitch and that Joe killed him just to help with this war that Charles was talking about," I said, "then I want to help you get Joe. He's gotta fall for that."

He nodded and walked away without saying another word. There was nothing else to say on it. I stood out in front of my apartment for a couple more minutes before going upstairs.

―

My bed was calling my name. I needed to close my eyes. It was happening fast and I had trouble keeping track of it in my head. When did it start to change? I lied down and my thoughts became heavy like my eyelids. With every blink, the past came back to me more and more clearly until I was back in that place where things weren't so serious and mistakes would bring only a smack to the back of the head, not a bullet.

There was this time, I'd say five summers back, when me and Chris were tight. We were like brothers. He wasn't slinging yet and I was just starting to come into my own as an athlete. I always had a basketball in my hands and Chris was always close behind me. We were walking down Fayette looking for some other people to play with. We loved running full court, but it was hard finding enough people to play. A lot of people we knew were more interested in hanging out on the corners.

"We're not gonna get nobody," Chris said, squinting because the sun was beaming down on us. "People are lazy. Plus this heat . . . "

"Come on," I said. "We gotta work on our games."

"We could try to get Byron and Petey," he said. "They'll play. At least we can run two-on-two."

"Aight," I said.

We found Byron and Petey a couple corners down on Fayette. They were both runners at that point—the people on the corner who served the drugs to the fiends after the money changed hands.

"Look at these two workin' men," Chris said as we walked up to the corner.

The two of them smiled when they saw us. The four of us shook hands. Bossman was blasting from the speakers of a parked car across from the corner.

"That's right," Byron said. "You two need to be out here gettin' stuff done instead of playin' a game."

He snatched the basketball out of my hands and I tried to get it back. He held it up in the air before tossing it to Petey.

"Gimme the ball," I said.

Petey threw the ball to me.

"I'm sayin'," Byron said, "Joe is gonna put me on the money soon."

"Fo' real?" Chris asked.

Byron nodded confidently.

"You two wanna play some two-on-two?" I asked.

"We can't," Byron said. "We gotta put in work here until it gets dark."

"You gotta be out here until dark?" I asked. "That's some crap."

"Nah," he said, pointing to his head. "It's smart. You think basketball or football is gonna take you up out of the hood, but it ain't. If you ain't slingin', you ain't nothin'."

"Whatever, man," I said.

Ordell, the corner chief, walked over and stood right next to us.

"What are you guys yappin' about?" he asked. "And you two, you're supposed to be workin'. What am I payin' you for?"

"There ain't no customers," Petey said.

"Well what do you do when there ain't no customers?" Ordell asked. "You walk up a few blocks and holler lookout. One of you go that way and the other one go that way." Ordell pointed in either direction from the corner.

Byron rolled his eyes, sighed, and started walking in one direction, and Petey went the other.

"And don't give me any attitude," Ordell said to Byron. "You ain't doin' me no favors."

We walked down the block with Byron. None of us said anything as we did. We stopped at Fayette and Brice. It was a dead corner.

"How do you deal with that stuff?" I asked.

"What?" Byron asked.

"People tellin' you what to do all the time?" I asked.

His eyes narrowed. "We can't all be like you," he said. "Our dads can't all work directly under Joe."

"My dad ain't even around," Chris said.

"What does that have to do with anything?" I asked.

Byron smirked right in my face.

"What?" I asked, getting closer to him.

"Nothing," he said. "Listen, I gotta work. If you two wanna stand out here with me and lookout for knockos, it's cool. But I can't play no ball. Not today."

Chris didn't say anything.

"Nah," I said. "We're gonna go play."

I started to walk away, and at first, Chris didn't follow. I turned around and eyed him. He looked over to Byron, put his head down, and finally caught up with me. We walked over to the park to play some one-on-one because there was no one else to play with.

Chris was no competition for me. We played three games and I won all three easily. I even skunked him once. He wasn't athletic like me. He was clumsy. He had no hands.

After our games, I shot free throws while he stood underneath the hoop and rebounded for me.

"Yo Marcus," he said. "You ever think that like, this is it? You know, West Baltimore?"

I took my three dribbles and put up the shot. Swish!

"I don't know, Chris," I said. "What do you mean?"

He threw the ball back to me.

"You got basketball and football," he said. "What do I got?"

"That's why I drag your lazy butt out here all the time," I said before taking another shot. Swish! "You gotta practice your game."

He held the ball. "Nah," he said. "This ain't for me. It's all you."

He threw the ball back to me again.

"Well what are you thinkin'?" I asked.

"I'm thinkin' of getting out on the corners," he said. "Start out like Byron and Petey, you know, as lookout, and then runner."

I stopped dribbling and eyed him. "You sure that's what you wanna do? You smart. Why not try getting a scholarship? Science or something?"

He shrugged his shoulders. "Come on, man," he said, "be real."

I took one last shot. Swish!

"It's gonna get dark soon," I said. "Can't see when there ain't no light."

We left the park and walked to my house. By the time we got there, the sun was halfway down and the sky was tinted orange. Mom and I lived in a row house near Fayette and Monroe. My dad stopped by every now and then, but not too much.

"You wanna come in and play some Playstation?" I asked.

"Yeah," he said.

Joe walked out of my front door. His eyes were serious and his hands were tense.

"Marcus?" he asked. "Where you been? I've been lookin' all around for you."

"We were just playin' a little ball," I said. "What's up?"

He looked down to Chris. "Why don't you run along," he said.

Chris stood there frozen. He looked at me.

"Whatchu lookin' at him for?" Joe asked. "Run along!"

Chris got the message and ran down to the end of the corner. He turned back to look at us before turning it.

"Marcus!" my mom yelled from inside the house. "Boy, where you been? Get in the damn house!"

"Cool out!" Joe yelled into the house. "I got him!" He put his arm around me. "Let's walk."

We walked down to the end of the corner and stopped. He smiled as he looked down at me. "You and *that* basketball," he said. "You always got that in your hands. And you're good at football, too. Damn. Maybe one day you'll be good enough to go pro. It'll take a lot of work, but it's possible."

I didn't say anything.

"You gotta stay in the house starting tomorrow, Marcus," he said. "It's not gonna be safe out on the streets for a while."

"What do you mean?"

"Nothin'," he said. "Just a little war. You don't need to be concerned with it."

"But I wanna play," I said. "It's the summer. I don't wanna be trapped in the house. And plus, I wanna work on my game."

He smiled at that. "It's just for a little while."

I caught a glimpse of his jeans; there were spots of red on them. The knuckles of his right hand were cut up too.

"Hopefully it won't take too long," he said.

"Is somebody snitching?" I asked.

"Boy," he said. "Ain't nobody say anything about snitching."

"People around the way always say that the drama comes when people snitch," I said.

"That's true," he said. "You don't ever want to be known as a snitch, hear?"

I nodded. We walked back down to my house.

"So you got me, right?" he asked when we got to my door. "Stay in the house, especially at night. I'll try to make this quick so you can get back out there and work on your game." He smiled.

I didn't say anything. I just looked down to the basketball in my hands.

His smile went away and his eyes became serious. "Hopefully the sports will work out for you, Marcus," he said. "So you don't gotta be out here."

I shrugged my shoulders.

"I'm gonna make sure that happens for you," he said. He put his hand out for a low five. I slapped it.

"Come on," he said. "You want some ice cream?"

I nodded. We walked back down the block and he put his arm around my shoulder.

———

When I got out of bed, I walked out to my living

room and it was dark. My mom was out and there wasn't any food in the fridge, just carryout menus from pizza spots and Chinese joints stuck to the front of it. I checked by the phone to see if my mom left me any messages, but mostly to see if Joe had sent word. He hadn't. There was one message from my mom—a note saying that both Coach Watson and Coach Jones had called for me.

I took the phone with me to the couch. I turned the TV on and put on the news. I didn't know why I put the news on, but with all that was going on with the war on West Baltimore's streets, I thought it made sense. There was nothing on there for me. There was always a war going on in West Baltimore. The only things that ever changed were the players. I turned off the TV and began to dial Coach Watson.

TWELVE

Coach Watson picked up after two rings. "Hello?" he said.

"Coach," I said.

"Marcus, where you been all day? I called the house three times."

I thought for a second. "I was out, Coach. Just getting to know the city."

"What do you mean?" he pressed.

"Just went to the Harbor. Wanted to get out of the west side for the day."

"Okay," he said.

There was a pause on the line.

"What's up?" I asked.

"Just wanted to see how you're doing with the suspension, and if you need to talk."

"I'm doing okay," I said.

There was another pause.

"Talk about what, Coach?" I asked.

"It's been a few days," he said. "I thought that maybe you were ready to tell me what that was all about the other night. I'm not trying bother you by bringing it up, but I think you owe it to yourself to tell somebody what happened."

"You mean I owe it to *you*?" I asked.

"No," he said. "You don't owe it to me. What happened the other night was a shock for everyone involved. I'm sure you're still shocked about it. I just think it'll help *you* to talk about it."

I took a deep breath on my side on the line.

"I know you, Marcus," he said. "You've allowed me to get close enough to know you and I appreciate that. I *know* that you've changed. And I know how much that game meant to you. I know how much your teammates mean to you. You care, Marcus.

I know you do. I also know how close you are to the streets. And it worries me."

My eyes started watering again. I pulled the phone away from my face. I didn't want Coach thinking that I was a wimp, crying and stuff. I *couldn't* let him know that I was so weak. I wiped my face on my sleeve, pulled myself together, and put the phone back up to my ear.

"Something happened out there on that field," he said. "Tell me, Marcus."

I thought about Joe and what he always said about snitching. It wasn't just Joe who talked about snitching, it was everybody. You could be a killer, hustler, or pimp in West Baltimore and still have more respect than if you were a snitch. But where was Joe now? Where were any of those guys from the corners? I was all alone carrying this crap. Byron and Coach Watson were the only two people I had. It's true that Joe's influence saved me from being expelled, but that wasn't enough. He hadn't checked up on me or even sent word. He wasn't there to ask me how I was doing with the suspension. *Screw Joe,* I thought to myself.

"You still there, Marcus?" Coach Watson asked.

"Yeah," I said. "Coach."

"Tell me what happened, Son."

"The linebacker," I said. "We were going back and forth the whole game. He was tough. A good player."

I paused. It was difficult for me to do what I was about to do. It was the hardest thing I ever had to do. It went against everything that I was ever taught and had seen out on the streets of West Baltimore. I took one more deep breath and then came out with it.

"He called me a 'nigger' twice," I said. "Once in the first half and then at the end of the game. I snapped after the second time."

Coach was silent on the other end.

"Coach?" I said.

"Yeah," he said. "Marcus."

"The fumble didn't help either," I said.

Coach chuckled at that and so did I.

"I'm sorry I let you and the team down," I said.

"You don't have to say that," he said. "Everyone fumbles."

"I'm not talking about the fumble," I said.

There was another pause on the line.

"I knew something like that happened," he said. "Why didn't you say something earlier? This would change everything, both in the newspapers and at school. You might not have been suspended if they knew the real reason you fought."

"It already happened," I said. "Can't do anything to change it now."

"That's not true," he said. "It'll change things. I can talk to Mr. Watkins—"

"No," I said. "Don't do that, Coach. Please."

"Okay," he said. "Okay, Marcus."

"Don't tell nobody, hear?" I said. "This is just for your ears."

"I won't," he said. "Call me anytime if you need

something or if you need to talk. I'll be there for you."

"Okay, Coach," I said. "Thanks."

"Good night, Son," he said.

"Good night, Coach."

I hung up the phone and looked down at the note that my mom had left for me. Coach Jones had called as well that day.

I picked the phone back up and dialed Coach Jones's number.

He picked up after three rings.

"Hello," he said.

"Coach Jones," I said. "It's Marcus. I'm returning your call."

"Yeah, Marcus," he said. "I just called to see if you are planning on staying in shape over the course of the suspension. Make sure you're running and doing drills while you have the time off. We need you to be ready to go by the time you get back to school."

I didn't say anything.

"We can't have you taking your time," he said, "getting back in shape."

"I'll be in shape," I said.

"Alright," he said. "I'll check in with you tomorrow or the next day. Take care of yourself."

I hung up the phone. Coach Jones was a lot different from Coach Watson. He didn't ask how I was carrying on with the suspension. Didn't ask about how I was dealing with the murder of an old friend. There was none of that. It was just business for Coach Jones. I understood that, and I understood that our relationship was different. I didn't judge him too hard for that.

I sat down on the couch in the living room. No TV. I wanted quiet. I felt a little better after talking to Coach Watson. I didn't feel like a snitch either.

THIRTEEN

I woke up around ten the next morning and my mom was still asleep. I showered, ate, and changed quickly. There were no calls. I had to go meet Byron on his corner to make plans for that night. He couldn't take off another day from running his corner—you'd have trouble if you did it more than once in a week. We would have to continue our investigation at night.

Before I left my apartment, I looked out of the window. The sky looked like a long, grey sheet. I grabbed my warmest hoodie along with gloves and a beanie, and I left the house.

I walked down Fayette Street toward Byron's

corner. He was leaning on the vacant house at the end of the block, the one that faced Fayette, while Petey, Melvin, and Little Rick were closer to the street. I shook hands and talked a little with the three of them before walking over to Byron. He lit a Newport. His eyes were tired and lifeless.

"What up, B?" I said as we shook hands. "You look burnt."

"Ain't had a wink of sleep in days, man," he said as he took a drag.

"What's going on out here?" I asked, nodding to the corner. There weren't any fiends out. I really didn't even see any as I walked down Fayette.

"Things are dead," he said.

"Chris's and Peanut's deaths still bringing heat?"

"Another guy dropped late last night over on Paca," he said before spitting on the sidewalk. "That's why we all the way over here in the middle of nowhere. Fiends know that West Side is hot right now with these bodies and they're heading to East Side to cop."

"Who fell last night?"

"Some guy," he said, and then flicked his cigarette into the street.

"You know him?"

He shook his head.

I looked over to Petey, Melvin, and Little Rick. They were quiet too.

"Guess what though?" he said.

I nodded.

"Word is that East Siders dropped the boy last night."

"Joe's war," I said. "Just like that guy Charles said."

Byron nodded and then looked past me. He looked like he was pissed off at the world—pissed off that he couldn't make any money on a dead corner and pissed off about Chris. There was no hope written on his face. He was about to do something crazy. I knew it by looking at his eyes. Over the years, I saw a lot of people out on those corners with the same dead look, and it never ended well for them.

"What's up for tonight?" I asked.

"My man's ready to meet," he said. "Ten o'clock at the bar near the harbor."

"The cop bar again?"

"Yeah."

"Can you tell me about it now?"

He shook his head. I didn't want to press him. I didn't feel like getting into a confrontation. It was too cold, plus my stomach was all sideways. I just stood next to him in silence with my hands in my pockets.

"We find out tonight," he said, breaking the silence. "We should go looking for Joe right after."

"That's another thing," I said. "It's gonna be hard to find him. Especially if he's getting ready for a war."

"I know."

We stood in silence again.

"Why don't you go ahead and dip out, man,"

he said. "Ain't nothin' going on around here today. I'll meet you at your crib around nine."

I nodded and started to walk towards Petey, Melvin, and Little Rick, but turned back around to face Byron.

"We should probably go separately," I said. "Just meet there."

Byron smiled. "What? you paranoid?"

"Just makes sense to do it that way."

"Aight," he said. "One other thing: try and think of all the spots Joe ever took you to. I know he's looked out for you over the years. He could be hiding out at one of the spots and you might know where it is."

I nodded and he shook another Newport out of his pack, popped it into his mouth, and bent down to put fire to it.

"Yo, B," I said. "Watch your back, hear?"

"Yeah, you too, Marcus," he said. "See you a little later."

I turned around and walked over to Byron's

three corner-boys. After talking with them about the events of the state championship game—Little Rick said that once the brawl jumped off, he hopped down onto the field and knocked out "at least ten white boys"—we all agreed that we couldn't wait for the summer and how it was too cold out there on the streets. I shook hands with all three of them and left. They had to stay out in the cold and wait for the fiends. I walked back to my apartment and when I entered, my mom already had the heater cooking.

———

I went straight to my room and took a nap. My mom was in her room and I didn't hear her TV on. She was sleeping. I slept until about eight o'clock that night. When I got up, I took a shower and changed into some warm clothes.

I went into the living room and saw my mom sitting on the couch with a beer in front of her.

We didn't speak to each other. The volume on the TV was turned up loud, but she wasn't paying attention to that either. She was looking through a magazine instead. I went over to the phone to see if there were any messages. Coach Jones called again. I balled up the paper and tossed it in the trash can. I looked in the fridge for something to eat only to find leftover carry-out again. My stomach turned and I shut the fridge.

I walked over to the couch, black Timberlands in hand, and sat down next to my mom. She had a lit Newport in one hand and her beer in the other. She eyed me as she took a long swig.

I fit one foot into a boot and tied the laces.

"Where you going?" she said.

"Out."

She rolled her eyes. "Don't get in no more trouble, hear? That ice up underneath you is thin."

I didn't respond. I just put my other boot on and tied the laces.

"Don't screw up your future, Marcus," she said.

"You got people countin' on you. Don't let us down."

I cut my eyes at her. "Who?" I said with a nod. "Joe?"

She didn't say anything to that.

I stood up from the couch.

"Joe hasn't called these last few days," I said.

She looked up at me with serious eyes. "You see the messages? I wanted you to get at him about the package."

I nodded. "When he gets in touch, I will. He's probably busy right now."

"Probably," she said before going back to her magazine.

The TV was so loud I thought my ear drums would explode. My mom only cared about getting more stuff. That was what moved her. She wasn't concerned for me. I mean, not really. She just saw me as her ticket—with sports, with Joe—It didn't matter to her *how* she got it. It was *that* she got it.

I grabbed the remote from the coffee table.

"Can you turn this crap down?" I asked.

She ripped the remote out of my hand.

"Leave it!" she said. "I like it that way."

"Bye Mom," I said.

"Bye Baby."

I took my heavy black coat and put it on. I did the same with my gloves and beanie and left the house.

———

When my feet hit Fayette, the cold air was already stinging my face. I zipped up my jacket as far as it could go to stop the chill from getting down into my bones. I needed to grab another pop-up taxi to get downtown and I needed to get out of the cold quick.

I waited on the corner with two fingers up. A few blocks away, there was an ambulance, two cop cruisers, and a crowd of people. Something had popped off on Mount and Fayette. Someone else had been hit in Joe's war. I dropped the two fingers out of the air and made my way over to see what was up. As I got closer to the crowd, I could see that my instinct was right. Somebody had been hit.

Petey and Melvin were at the edge of the circle. I tapped Petey on the back and both of them turned to face me. Petey's eyes were red and wet, Melvin's were angry. Little Rick was nowhere to be found.

"What's going on?" I asked.

"They got B," Petey said in a low voice.

"Byron?" I asked. "Byron is in that bag over there?"

I looked over to the spot where the paramedics were zipping up the white body bag. They were getting ready to lift it up and take it away in the ambulance.

I grabbed Petey by the shoulders. "Tell me that's not Byron in there!" I said loudly, but not loud enough to draw attention. "Tell me you're messin' with me, man!"

Petey put his head down and shook it. Melvin

kept eying the body bag and mumbling something to himself.

I let go of Petey and got up close to him.

"When?" I asked.

"'Bout an hour ago," Melvin said.

"We closed up shop early," Petey said. "Wasn't much business today."

"East Side guys," Melvin said.

"What?" I asked.

"It's East Side guys that are droppin' all our soldiers," Melvin said. "We fittin' to tool up and go over there and handle some business."

Melvin quickly lifted his hoodie to reveal the butt of his semi-automatic and then covered it up again.

"Where's Little Rick?" I asked.

"He went home to pack up his heat," Melvin said. "He wants to go over there *tonight*."

Petey just kept his head down.

Two of the paramedics lifted the body bag onto the stretcher and slowly wheeled it over to the ambulance. The two cops in uniform were standing and talking to the two men in suits. They were the murder police. They were looking out to the crowd as the uniformed cops talked to them.

I had to go. I broke off from the crowd and walked down Mount and didn't stop walking until it was quiet. Joe got Byron. And if I knew anything about Joe, I was next. He might've even had someone watching my apartment, following me, I didn't know.

I stopped at an intersection that had some traffic and put two fingers up again. A pop-up cab stopped after a few minutes. The driver rolled his window down.

"Where to?" he asked.

"Downtown," I said. "Harbor."

He nodded to the backseat and I opened the door and climbed in.

FOURTEEN

I walked into the cop bar without hesitation. It was too cold out there to screw around. The spot was packed this time. All cops. Some were in uniforms, some weren't. I didn't know who I was looking for. I just hoped that whoever it was knew to look for me. I definitely didn't fit in. Anybody could take one look at me and label me an outsider. I stood close to end of the bar looking into the crowd, trying not to stare too hard. After five minutes, a white man in a suit got up from a booth in the back, the same booth that Byron, Charles, and I sat at the day before. He walked over and slid in at the bar right next to me. I could hear his drink order—a shot of Jameson and a beer. After he got his drinks, he turned to me.

"You Marcus?" he asked.

I nodded.

"Follow me."

I followed him to the back booth. We weaved through a thick crowd of cops who were having a good time. They didn't blink twice as I walked by with the man wearing a suit.

He stopped at the booth and sat down. I sat across from him.

"Where's your friend?" he asked.

He was an older cop, and from the look of his outfit, probably a detective. I could see all the lines in his forehead. His tired eyes followed mine as I thought of what to say.

"He's gone," I said.

The man held his shot glass up to his lips in shock. He didn't take a sip. He put it down on the table.

"What do you mean, 'gone'?"

"Just like it sounds," I said.

He didn't say anything to that. He let it ride. We sat there listening to the party going on around us. I didn't even know what I was doing there. Without Byron, I was lost and alone.

"So you're Byron's proof?" I asked.

"Excuse me?"

"You're the man who was gonna tell us that our friend was no snitch."

"Chris?"

I nodded.

"I can prove it," he said. "I'm the one working the case and there's no record of your friend Chris being taken into custody recently, and he's never made a recorded statement about Joe Milsap."

"Why are you helping Byron?" I asked, then caught myself. "I mean, why were you helping him?"

He took his shot and a bitter look came onto his face. He sighed as the poison went down.

"Why are you helping me?" I asked.

"Because I'm trying to nail Joe. And people out there are trying to help me," he said. "Byron was going to give me information on Joe in exchange for me giving him information about your friend Chris."

I tried to study his face, to see if there was any hatred in his eyes or to figure out if he was messing with me. But I didn't find it. All I saw was his tired eyes. It all started to make sense. Byron was ready to go out. He knew he was getting ready to talk to the police, and after that, his life would be over. He figured he could just go after Joe until the streets caught up with him for talking to the police.

"How'd you get to Byron?" I asked.

"I got his name from another informant that I'm working with," he said. "The man told me that Byron wasn't very happy with the way Joe is running his corners and that he was ready to speak on Joe."

I knew who this "informant" was. Charles was talking to the police too. I could see everything clearly. For all the talk out there about snitching and staying tight with your crew, there was this part of it too—the *real* part. They never said anything about this part out on the corners, about how all the talk of loyalty is just talk. When a guy's neck is on the line, you best believe he's gonna talk to the police about everything and everybody. He'll do anything to keep himself out of jail, anything that will get him a deal.

"You don't know anything about Joe Milsap, do you?" he asked.

I shook my head. "Just what everyone else around the way knows."

His shoulders slumped. "And that is?"

"That he's the king of West Baltimore."

I stood up from the booth.

"Hey, Marcus," he said. "Who was that Chris kid to you?"

"We grew up together," I said.

"He didn't look like a bad kid, just sold a little drugs. No violent stuff. Any idea what happened?"

"We lost touch a few years back," I said. "I'm just tryin' to . . . I'm just tryin' to figure things out myself."

He nodded and took a big sip of beer. "I was at the championship game the other night," he said. "What the hell happened out there?"

"Just not my time, I guess."

"You gotta keep that temper in check," he said. "Especially where *you* live. That'll get you killed."

I nodded to him, turned, and left the bar. Outside, I caught the first taxi I saw—a real one, not a pop-up—and gave the driver the address to my apartment. I looked out the window as we drove across town over to the west side. It was one of those bitter, cold nights where you can smell snow in the air. I knew what I had to do. I couldn't get to Joe myself. There was no way now that he was coming for me. There was only one chance.

"Yo!" I called up to the driver. "That address I gave you before. Don't go there. I need to go somewhere else."

"Still West Baltimore?" he asked.

"Yeah," I said. "It's off Edmonson. Edmonson and Pulaski."

He shrugged his shoulders and drove a little further than he expected down into the west side.

FIFTEEN

I didn't leave the house for the next three days. The window in my room had a clear view of the street in front of my building. I looked out of it constantly, trying to figure out if Joe had anyone watching my apartment, but I didn't notice anything strange. My mom didn't seem to think it was weird that I never left the house. She was too busy staying out late with her friends, even though I told her to stay in for fear of Joe getting to her. My sleep during those nights was choppy at best. I kept having this dream where I heard the front door to the apartment open followed by footsteps. And then either

Joe or Sheik would walk into my room without any emotion on their face and shoot me in the chest.

But the real thing never came.

———

My suspension was up. It was time for me to go back to school and join the basketball team. The night before I was allowed back at school, I called Coach Watson and told him that we needed to talk. He came over and I told him everything about Byron, Charles, and the detective. He told me that he'd watch out for me and that he would be there in the morning to give me a ride to school.

The next morning, I got myself ready for school while my mom was still fast asleep. I showered, changed into a new outfit, and had breakfast— cereal again. While I waited for Coach Watson, I went to the front door and picked up the copy of *The Baltimore Sun* that was always there in the mornings. We rarely read the paper. The only time my mom even looked at it was to cut out articles about me from the sports section. Usually, the copies of the *Sun* piled up outside our door or inside on the dining room table, until they were eventually tossed in the garbage can. On that morning though, I decided to get the paper and open it up. I had plenty of things to look out for.

First, I looked for any articles on Joe. I wanted to see if that detective had any luck finding others to give up information on Joe's "business" on the west side. There was nothing in there on Joe.

Then I looked for an article on Byron's murder and found it—a tiny paragraph in the back of the Metro section that mentioned Byron's death was "drug-related" and not much else.

Next, I checked the sports section to see if there was anything on me. There was a small announcement in the high school section letting the city know that their favorite local football and basketball star was going back to school today. The paper quoted Coach Jones as saying that he couldn't wait to get me "back into the school's halls and on the right track."

The last thing that caught my eye was the front-page article in the sports section. It was concerned with the city's growing number of racially charged fights between black and white high school sports teams. There were four high school brawls in Baltimore sports during the last month—two in boys' basketball, one in girls' basketball, and the one I was involved in. The one thing that the three basketball brawls had in common was that they all started after a white player called a black player a "nigger." No one from the *Sun* talked to me. They didn't say how the brawl started in the state football championship game, but I'm sure they had a pretty good idea. The article finished with a warning. It warned that there would be more security at the games from then on and that participation in a fight would bring on a full-season suspension, no questions asked.

I folded the newspaper and put it down on the

dining room table. It was time to go back to school. It was time to play ball again.

When Coach Watson picked me up in front of my building, I looked in every direction as I walked to his car. There was no one out there waiting on me except for Coach.

"Hey Marcus," he said.

"Hey Coach."

"Listen, Marcus," he said. "We're going right now to the western district police station to tell them about all this stuff with Joe."

"They already know all about him," I said.

"I mean, that he's after *you*."

"All this could just be paranoia," I said. "If he wanted me, he could've had me by now."

"You're probably right," he said. "But just to be safe?"

"I have a feeling that things are gonna be fine, Coach."

"How can you be sure?" he asked.

"It's just, growing up here, seeing all this, you kind of know when it's your time to go."

I smiled at him. I don't really know why I did.

He looked back at me with sincerity in his eyes. I wasn't used to a whole lot of people in my life looking at me that way.

"It just doesn't feel like my time," I said.

He nodded and we sat in silence for about a minute. He started the car and drove down Fayette toward the school.

———

The basketball team had already started the regular season during the week I was suspended from school. The team played four games without me that week, going undefeated without much of a challenge in any of the games.

Coach Jones wasted no time easing me back in.

"You're gonna start tonight," he said in the locker room about an hour before the game.

I smiled and shook my head.

"Are you sure?" I asked, sitting in front of my locker. "I mean, the guys have been playing well. Do you think I deserve to start?"

"You're our best defender," he said. "And I don't believe in rust. Besides, I need you back in shape as fast as possible. Our schedule is about to get tougher. Way tougher."

"Okay Coach."

Coach Jones walked out of the locker room toward his office. Errol passed by him on his way in and I nodded to him. He sat down next to me.

We shook hands.

"What's up, Marcus?" he said.

"Good to be back," I said. "For real."

"Yeah, it wasn't the same around here without you."

"It's funny," I said. "I thought I needed a break after football, especially with the way things ended."

He nodded.

"But just that one day before school, running up

and down the court with you and the rest of the guys," I nodded to my teammates around the locker room, "that stuff made me feel safe. Being on the basketball court. Being on the football field. A guy don't feel safe like that often in this city."

"I feel you," he said. "We're glad that you're back."

We shook again.

"Now let's go handle some business," he said.

"Let's do it," I said.

Twenty minutes before the game, Coach Jones warned us about fighting with the other team. He made a point to remind us that we were going against a mostly-white private school that night and that we had to ignore any taunts out there on the court, even if they included the magic word.

Coach pulled me aside in the locker room right before we hit the floor.

"You heard what I said, right?" he asked.

"Yeah," I said. "The fight didn't happen because

of a racial slur. I was pissed that I fumbled the game away. Lost my cool. Won't happen again."

"There's always gonna be mistakes made out there, Marcus. That can't be an excuse," he said. "What happens when something goes wrong out there for you tonight? What are you gonna do?"

"I'll just make sure to slap one of my own teammates in the back of the head instead of one them white boys on the other team," I said.

He didn't find any humor in that.

"Just give me your word," he said.

"You have my word."

Coach Jones left me there in the locker room and I took a minute before I went out with the rest of my team. The fact that Coach Jones hadn't picked up on my lie about the brawl told me a lot about Coach Watson. It's not that I had any doubts; it's just that it was hard for me to trust. Coach Watson had my back. He wasn't just saying it. He would protect me.

I took the floor with the starting line up and it didn't feel strange being out there after the long break from basketball. The court was my home in the winter, just like the football field was home in the fall. Those two places probably felt more like home than my actual home.

After the ball was tossed up and the game started, I was so hyped up that I couldn't breathe after a few possessions. I had to ask out of the game after two minutes. I took a seat on the bench and tried to calm myself. I took five deep breaths, and as usual, it worked. That made me think of Joe. Ever since I started playing varsity ball—football and basketball—Joe never missed a home game and was always sitting in the front row with my mom and Sheik. But when I looked into the front row that night, I only saw my mom with two empty seats to her left.

We took a quick ten-point lead early in the game.

It was okay for my mind to wander a little. I kept looking to the two empty seats next to my mom. Maybe my plan had worked. Or maybe Joe wasn't really coming after me and it was all in my head. Then my eyes went to my mom. I wanted things to change in our relationship. I knew that change would be hard, but I didn't want her depending on Joe for money anymore. I didn't want that hanging over us anymore.

If I could just focus on ball, I could go to college and then maybe the pros. Then *I* could take care of my mom without someone having to get hurt or strung out for it. But I needed a clear head to do that—a clear head and a clear heart. And even if I didn't make the pros, a college degree would be enough to get us out of the west side.

Coach Jones put me back in the game at the beginning of the second quarter. We had a fifteen-point lead. Now that the butterflies were out of me and I had control of my wind, I could just play. It was just a game. And it was fun. I was rusty, but it didn't matter. I played hard on defense like I always I did, getting a few steals and a couple of blocks, and I was a beast on the boards, pulling down seven rebounds in the second quarter alone.

We went into the locker room up twenty at the half. I hadn't scored yet, but no one cared. Errol came over and gave me a pat on the back of the head in the locker room, and that meant a lot. I could learn a lot about being the leader of a team just by watching him. He appreciated how hard I played and that made me want to play even harder. I would definitely copy some of his leadership skills and take them to the football field the following fall.

Coach Jones walked over to me during halftime.

"How are you feeling?" he asked.

"Aw," I said. "It was crazy at first. I couldn't get any air."

"Too hyped."

"It felt normal again, after that."

"Even though we're up by a lot," he said, "I'm gonna play you more in the second half. We're playing Gilman Prep at the end of the week. We're gonna need the real you in that one."

I nodded. "That's cool, Coach."

Just like in the first half, there wasn't much drama during the second. No brawls. Not even a racial slur. I played the whole third quarter and scored early. I finished the game with ten points, twelve rebounds, five steals, and four blocks. The highlight of the game came at the end of the third when I dunked with one hand on the other team's tallest player—a slow-footed, seven-footer. He didn't know what hit him. Our crowd went crazy after that, raining down taunts to the poor kid for the rest of the game. For what it's worth, I helped him up off the floor after the play and told him that it happens to everybody.

We won by thirty points.

It felt good being on the bench with my team-mates in the fourth quarter. I was glad to be a part of something again—something that mattered, something real.

SIXTEEN

After the game, I took my time showering and changing. I wanted to think on it, all of it.

I was surprised to see my mom waiting for me outside the locker room. She was the only one out there. All of my teammates had already left with their families.

She gave me a big hug and kiss on the cheek when I walked over to her. She smeared some of her bright red lipstick on there for good measure. And even though no one was there watching us, a feeling of embarrassment hit me as she wiped it off.

"You did good, Baby," she said.

"Thanks, Mom."

A few moments of silence passed.

"Joe wasn't up in the stands?" I asked, even though I knew the answer.

"No," she said.

I just wanted to see if she heard anything up there in the stands. You could always hear about what's going on in the streets at a high school sports event in West Baltimore. Maybe she wasn't listening close enough.

"You want a ride?" she asked.

"Nah, I'm gonna catch one with Coach Watson," I said. "We gotta talk."

"Okay, Baby," she said. "I'm gonna have something real special for dinner when you get home."

I smiled. "Something special" really meant that my mom was ordering Chinese that night, instead of pizza or subs.

"Thanks, Mom," I said. "I appreciate it."

"No doubt, Baby."

We hugged again and she was on her way. I truly did appreciate her saying that she would have dinner ready for me at home. That was no joke. I knew a lot of people in West Baltimore who didn't have a hot meal waiting at home for them.

The reason I told my mom that I would catch a ride home with Coach Watson was because he wanted to talk some more about Joe and me going to the police. I didn't really want to talk on it any more, but Coach Watson was my guy. If he wanted to talk, we'd talk.

I was in the back parking lot waiting for coach Watson when someone walked up from behind and tapped me on the shoulder. It was quiet and the lighting was bad back there. I was the only one outside; everyone else was long gone after the game ended. I thought that this could be it. Joe had finally caught up with me, or maybe it was Sheik. I had a thought, briefly, that maybe it *was* my time.

I turned around slowly, and when I saw that it was Petey, all the air rushed out of my body. He wasn't wearing the same face as the night Byron was killed. He looked happy and his wide smile scared me more than anything.

"What up, Petey?" I said.

"What's going on, Marcus?"

We shook hands.

I didn't know what to say, so I let him come with it.

"You dunked all over that white boy!" he said, copying the move, except he was me and I was the unfortunate white boy.

"You were at the game?" I asked.

"Yeah, you balled out," he said.

"I didn't know you were coming," I said.

He clapped his hands together and blew into them for warmth. His breath shot out of his mouth and floated up into the air.

"Just wanted to let you know that the information you gave us on Joe, all of it, was right," he said. "And it's taken care of. None of it will come back on you."

I leaned in close to him and talked low. "You mean . . . ?"

He nodded. "The night Byron got dead, Little Rick was all ready to go to war with the East Side guys. But you came with the information and when it all checked out, Little Rick changed his target."

"Little Rick got Joe?"

He nodded again, this time with more excitement in his eyes. "Got Sheik too." He put his right hand up and molded it into the form of a gun. He kicked it up twice to mimic the action of shots fired.

"How?" I asked. "How did Little Rick get close to Joe?"

"Sheik is Rick's godfather. He got to them that way."

"Rick did his own godfather?"

"Hey, Marcus, you know how it is out here," he said. "Byron and Chris, they was a part of the crew. We was all a part of the crew. We stood out on those corners together in the heat and in this cold. Joe and Sheik, they was far away from the corners, but still tryin' to make moves out there. They had to fall."

"Did Rick find out if Joe was after me?" I asked.

Petey looked over my shoulder. I turned around to see that Coach Watson was coming over to us.

"It's all good, Marcus," he said as he started to back away. "You don't gotta worry about nothin' anymore."

"Watch yourself out there, Petey," I said.

"You too, my dude," he said. "We all watchin' you—we countin' on you. You made an impact on the streets with that stuff with Joe. You did something out here."

And with that hanging in the air, he turned around and walked through the pale, orange parking lot and into the darkness of its edges.

"Marcus," Coach Watson said, "who was that?"

"Just an old friend from around the way."

"We should go to the western district station right now," he said. "You're not safe. Joe could—"

"It's all good, Coach Watson. It's Baltimore," I said, "Joe's gone. Things sorted themselves out."

He forced a smile and shook his head. "One more year, son. Just keep away from that stuff for one more year."

We got into his car, left the parking lot, and drove down Fayette toward my apartment. The corners and streets were quiet. It was cold out. There wasn't anything left to do that night but mourn the loss of a few more dead soldiers.